ENDG AME

ENDGAME

Jeffrey Round

DUNDURN
TORONTO

Editor: Shannon Whibbs
Design: Laura Boyle
Cover Design: Laura Boyle
Printer: Webcom
Image Credits: © Lucky Team Studio/ shutterstock.com
Author Photo: © Michael Erickson

Library and Archives Canada Cataloguing in Publication

Round, Jeffrey, author
      Endgame / Jeffrey Round.

Issued in print and electronic formats.
ISBN 978-1-4597-3325-1 (paperback).--ISBN 978-1-4597-3326-8 (pdf).--
ISBN 978-1-4597-3327-5 (epub)

      I. Title.

PS8585.O84929E53 2016   C813'.54   C2015-906344-2
                                                 C2015-906345-0

1   2   3   4   5   20   19   18   17   16

We acknowledge the support of the Canada Council for the Arts and the Ontario Arts Council for our publishing program. We also acknowledge the financial support of the Government of Canada through the Canada Book Fund and Livres Canada Books, and the Government of Ontario through the Ontario Book Publishing Tax Credit and the Ontario Media Development Corporation.

Care has been taken to trace the ownership of copyright material used in this book. The author and the publisher welcome any information enabling them to rectify any references or credits in subsequent editions.

— J. Kirk Howard, President

The publisher is not responsible for websites or their content unless they are owned by the publisher.

Printed and bound in Canada.

VISIT US AT
Dundurn.com | @dundurnpress | Facebook.com/dundurnpress | Pinterest.com/dundurnpress

Dundurn
3 Church Street, Suite 500
Toronto, Ontario, Canada
M5E 1M2

For all my friends — especially the crazy ones!

"Punk rock was an earthquake." — *Joe Strummer*

CHAPTER 1

Harvey Keill finished his lunch of oysters and Chivas Regal before moving on to the Krispy Kremes. He ate a cinnamon twist and pushed aside the unfinished box, licking the powdered sugar from his short, fat fingers. Next, he turned his attention to the morning's correspondence. Along with the usual unwanted flyers and bills lay an oversized envelope. Harvey noted the return address with satisfaction as he slit it open, read the letter, and tossed it on the desk with the rest of the mail.

He picked the envelope up again and shook it. A clear plastic CD case slid into his hands. No label, nothing to indicate what it might be. There was one more item inside, a photocopied newspaper clipping, which he unfolded carefully. As he did, a telltale sprinkle of white powder rained down on his green blotter. He *tsked* and brushed it in a little pile beside the doughnut box, wiping his hands on his pant legs.

Harvey straightened his cravat and spread the clipping across his desk, noting the headline: *Ladykillers Together Again?* The question mark worried him. Hadn't it all been arranged? No matter. That was probably just more media drama. In any case, *Noise* had been the perfect tabloid for the announcement. Everyone who was anyone in the music industry knew and respected it. And Harvey wanted *everyone* to know. After years of trying to engineer a get-together, it looked as though the impossible was finally set to unfold.

He sat back and read:

> A coup for fans! You too can be part of the sensational Ladykillers reunion tour. (See contest details page 59.)
>
> Since the popular punk-rock group broke up in the late nineties, fans have been begging for a comeback. It looks as though their dreams may come true.
>
> Founding members Spike Anthrax and Max Hardcore are said to be brokering a reunion later this month on Shark Island, a private retreat off the coast of Washington state. Singer Anthrax, who once vowed never to record with the band again, seems to have reconsidered.
>
> Shark Island has been the subject of much speculation of late. Insider sources suggest that either Madonna or Bono recently purchased the exclusive retreat, though spokesmen for those artists deny the claims. Other sources say the state government had been using the island for secret experiments.
>
> Ladykillers recorded a number of worldwide hits in the late eighties and nineties, but the group broke up amid financial and personal squabbles. Manager Harvey Keill was accused of defrauding members of their earnings, although those charges were dropped before the case made it to court.

Harvey sighed and sat back. After all these years, they persisted in making him look like a robber baron who preyed on innocent musicians. If only the media knew just how innocent the Ladykillers weren't.

They'd been solid gold for a while though, Harvey recalled, casting a glance around his office, with its rich leather uphol-stery and fine wood-grain furniture. Original artwork adorned the walls with some fancy names attached. A marble chess set sat in a far corner — a gift from Elvis Costello, though Costello never called anymore. Harvey seldom had visitors who played now. In fact, it was a while since anybody had been through those doors or bothered to contact him, apart from a few obsessed fans and a couple of diehard critics who still took the group's legacy seriously.

Though it was hard to admit, times had been lean since the band's breakup. Still, Spike and Max hadn't been his only claim to glory. Five framed gold records hung over his desk. None of them was by the Ladykillers. The world needed to remember that Harvey Keill had had other successes in his day.

He turned back to the clipping:

> Pete Doghouse, the original Ladykillers bassist, is also confirmed for the lineup. Rumours are rife as to who will replace the group's drummer, Kent Stabber, who died of a drug overdose in 1999. In its heyday, the band had a history of reputed drug use and was once implicated in the death of a fan who died of an ecstasy overdose at a CD release party.
>
> Speaking on behalf of the group, Keill said the band "are anxious to put those days behind them and prove that they are what they've always been — just a fun-loving bunch of guys who want noth-ing more than to please their fans and make great music."
>
> And it looks as though that's set to happen. Turn to page 59 for details on how to enter this exciting contest and your chance to sit in on a history-making reunion!

Harvey reached for another doughnut. More of the white powder stained his blotter as he bit into the soft core. His thoughts drifted. Sure, he'd helped himself to a few dollars now and again. Who wouldn't have, in his position? Nobody else could have made stars out of those talentless humanoid grunts. Where would they have been without him? Nowhere. Or worse, stuck in Spokane getting by on petty thefts. Or, more likely, they'd have graduated to robbing banks by now.

Still, they knew better than to complain about Harvey Keill. They'd done worse in their time. Far worse. Fortunately for them, Harvey had been there to protect them from the consequences. But even after all that, they still turned on him in the end. Moronic ingrates. As if he'd ever let them get the better of him.

He stood and went to the side table, pondering his chessboard. All it had taken to get the band to drop the charges against him was a little reminder about a certain past indiscretion. They'd run quickly enough with their tails between their legs. It hadn't entirely stopped the grumbling, though. So it was time to do something about that once and for all. He'd already thought long and hard about what he would say and do when he got them all together again.

Harvey picked up the white knight and moved it forward till it threatened the black king of his imaginary opponent. "Check," he said to the empty room.

He ambled over to his stereo and slipped the unlabelled CD into the player. After a few seconds, a twanging guitar started up. Harvey recognized the Ladykillers' popular anthem, "The Twelve Days of Shagging." Spike Anthrax's nasal rasp erupted from the speakers: "On the first day of shagging, my true love gave to me a love song full of hate … "

A love song full of hate. A grin spread across Harvey's face. This was going to be a pleasure. It was all set to happen just as he'd planned. Yes, indeed — it was long past time to settle some old scores.

CHAPTER 2

Spike Anthrax looked out at the Washington coastline. A blue sky was dotted with sharp-edged clouds. Fall colours had settled in the trees on his right. On the left, the white-capped waves of the Pacific swept the shore. Some would have said it made a pretty scene. Spike couldn't care less. The train rattled along, making a soft lulling sound. The station was just an hour away.

With his green-streaked hair and a worn dog collar around his neck, he looked like a page out of history. Punk-rock history. As he put his feet up on the recliner across from him, an old woman gave him a disapproving look.

"Those poor seats don't deserve to be treated like that," she said.

Spike raised his fists to his eyes, as if to hide his tears. He left them there long enough for her to see his tattoos: *S-T-A-R* on his right hand knuckles and *R-A-T-S* mirroring it on the left. He opened his eyes. She was still staring.

"Boo-hoo. Poor seats," he said with a sneer.

He waited till she turned to look out the window then pulled the letter from his jacket pocket, unfolding it and smoothing the creases. After all these years, to hear from Harvey Keill. The unbelievable gall of the man! What was he after — forgiveness? If so, he'd never get it.

Spike reread the letter carefully to catch the tone of the words:

> *My Dear Elyot:*
>   *I hope this finds you well and prospering*
> *after all these years.*

Spike snorted. Nobody else called him Elyot anymore. Not even his own mother. That was Harvey all over. Mr. Pompous Asshole. He probably still stuffed himself on doughnuts and wore those stupid cravats and pondered his chessboard like the upper-crust twat he'd always pretended to be. When he and the other band members met back in Spokane, they'd all been poor as shit. Not a pedigree or a penny between them. Not now, though. And certainly not Harvey. He'd become the rich pompous bastard he always pretended to be.

Spike's eye ran down the page.

> *There's been far too much water under the*
> *bridge. They say to let bygones be bygones, but*
> *I've always felt you were given short shrift back*
> *in the glory days of the Ladykillers.*

What a joke! Spike thought. *Short shrift indeed.* As far as Spike was concerned, he'd never been thoroughly compensated for all that music. And great fucking music it was, too!

> *That's what comes of bringing lawyers into these*
> *affairs, of course. I warned everyone about it*
> *then. Nevertheless, I feel it's time to make*
> *amends and — dare I say — to make up? It's*
> *time to get over what happened, Elyot. I'm sure*
> *you feel the same as me. (You always were the*
> *sensible one.)*

*As you can see, I've arranged a little
get-together for the band — a reunion, if you
like. It's time to take advantage of the group's
legendary name. (I've heard rumours you'll be
inducted into the Rock 'n' Roll Hall of Fame
next year if the votes are there. Just between us,
I fully intend to make that happen if I have to
pay for the votes myself, but more on that later.)*

Spike stopped to ponder this. The Rock 'n' Roll Hall of Fame.
That would cap things off nicely. And about fucking time, too.
Nobody respected genius anymore. It was time to prove that
Spike Anthrax was no has-been. He'd show them all who was
still the king.

*Yes — I can hear you saying it's time for the
rewards. And maybe more, if you'd let me compensate you personally. Informally, of course. A
little something between friends. I can't preju-
dice myself in the eyes of the law. (This will have
to stay between us, is what I'm saying.)*

When the letter arrived, Spike wondered if Harvey really
expected to be taken seriously. It smelled like another publicity
stunt. God knows he'd been good at engineering them. Publicity
stunts and broken promises — that was Harvey's style. But the
bastard lived in high style, if the rumours were to be believed, so if
Harvey was offering to pay him something on the side … well then,
by god, he'd be taken seriously. Spike Anthrax would come around,
as requested, to receive his just deserts. There'd be no stopping him.

*Dare I say it's time to finish that last album?
Endgame smacked of genius, Elyot. You knew*

*it. I knew it. We all knew it. I can't tell you how
pained I was when you decided not to finish
it, though I understand your reasoning. But it
still can stand as a testament to your greatness,
if you're willing.*

*If you agree it's time, then join me with Max
and Pete, plus a few others at a little retreat off
the coast of Seattle. I'll keep the name of our special patron a secret till I get there. Everything's
arranged. Just follow the instructions at the end
of this letter. We'll all be there. Don't disappoint
us, Elyot, old pal.*

*For the old times. For fame and glory. For
the Ladykillers!*

*Yours ever,
Harvey*

Spike stopped to consider. Maybe Harvey was right — it
was time to let bygones be bygones. If there was anything left
to share between the remaining band members, hadn't they
better do it while they could? Kent was already gone. Who'd be
next? Still, he couldn't believe Max Hardcore would agree to a
reunion. The bastard hated everyone's guts. That son of a bitch
was the ultimate punk-rock bad guy. Max used to laugh at all
those bands that got back together for lucre.

Die young and keep a pretty corpse. Piss in the face of life.
That was what they'd all agreed on back then. Better to go out
in one great, pestiferous bang than rot away in some rosy-hued
pasture looking back on your past glories.

But back then they'd been on top of the game. Now … now
was different. None of them had expected to live this long. None
of them thought they'd be around to contemplate what it meant

to be a rock 'n' roll legend without a recording contract at fifty. What good was fame? You couldn't eat it or pay your bloody mortgage with it. The most it ever did was get you laid any time you wanted, which had been plenty back then. Now was another story, though. Now, your back did you in half the time when exhaustion didn't drive you to bed before ten o'clock at night.

Some fucking legend.

The clipping had clinched it for Spike Anthrax, a.k.a. Elyot Jones. There, in black and white, was an article from *Noise*, the best damn music magazine ever. Above it was a picture of the band in their prime. So what if that shit-heap of a tabloid had trashed the group in its heyday, making them out to be derivative, untalented losers? They'd come round at last. No such thing as bad press, Harvey always said. Besides, the controversy fuelled by the lousy reviews helped propel more than one album up the charts. The fans had been crazy for them even when the critics sharpened their knives on them. But this piece — *Ladykillers Together Again?* — had the whiff of success. So Harvey was at it once more, stirring the flames. Who said the glory days were over?

Yes, Spike told himself, *this is too good to pass up. And about fucking time. You could kick a genius like Spike Anthrax in the teeth — lots of people had — but you can't keep him down forever.*

It still pained him when he thought about the band and all the fun they'd had. All the dirty good times they'd shared. It was time to live a little again and, yes, to let bygones be bygones. Once he'd settled a few scores, of course.

Spike glanced up. The old bitch had crawled off to bother someone else in another part of the coach. Piss on her. He looked out the window. They'd passed Seattle a while ago. Soon, he'd be on a boat bound for Shark Island and the return of everything he had missed all these years. Special patron, huh? He'd heard the rumours: Madonna, everyone said. Her music was shite, but she had clout by the bucketful.

Good old Harvey.

Still, before he agreed to anything — even to finishing *Endgame* — Harvey Keill was going to hear what Spike Anthrax had to say on the subject of unpaid royalties and the neglected genius of punk-rock superstars.

CHAPTER 3

T he train rounded a corner as the whistle blew overhead in a high-pitched whine. Verna Temple checked her makeup in the compact mirror. She was nearing forty, but most people took her for a decade younger. She made a pert *moue*, pouting at her reflection as she licked a spot of lipstick off a tooth. Those lips were something to behold. Full and red, as if they'd been stung by bees into a plump, round smoothness. Two quick injections and *voila!* Perfect for life. She smoothed a platinum lock across her brow. It was funny how she'd become such an old-fashioned sort of girl. Not at all what anyone would have predicted.

She picked up the magazine in her lap and turned the pages: Taylor Swift, William and Kate, more Taylor Swift. Miley Cyrus, Justin Bieber, George Clooney, and One Direction. She knew them all. The faces changed, but the news was the same: romance, marriage, betrayals, drug abuse, babies, divorce. A column called "Toxic Love" caught her interest briefly — she was an old hand at that — and on the next page an ad for Sexi-Nitee. All the usual trash glittering at the bottom of the barrel.

The waters of Puget Sound twinkled up ahead. Verna watched the craggy hills approach. She hadn't been to the west coast since she was a child, on one of those endless car trips with her parents and her younger brother. The experience hadn't been so great. Nor were the memories. She had Bill and Audrey to thank for that, of course. It had turned out to be another one of their drinking and arguing binges. Not much as parents went, that's for sure. Sometimes she wondered how they were — or if they were even still alive. But these days she wondered less and less about them. Her brother had been a total shit, of course. He always was, but you don't speak ill of the dead, Verna reminded herself.

The past was past. And what you couldn't change, you put behind you. That was another thing Verna knew. She'd done plenty of putting behind her in her time. What you didn't like or couldn't live with, you could reinvent. That was her credo. From that poor, homely creature she'd once been had come the ultimate femme fatale: Marilyn Redux. All the right curves and moves.

Since leaving home, her life had been a balancing act of sobering fact and startling fantasy, of harsh truths and the little white lies she told to make it through the day. She couldn't afford a slip, not even in the things others took for granted: the stories about her mother and father, about her brother, even her work history. She rehearsed them carefully until she was exactly what and who she claimed. No more and no less. No ripple, no shimmer of doubt to mar the surface of the image she had so carefully built up all these years. If anyone looked for the person she'd once been, they would never find her. Those days were long gone. With any luck, the memories would be better on this trip.

Verna tucked her compact back in her purse and looked up. The woman sharing her compartment had got on somewhere south of Seattle, but they hadn't said a word past a quick hello. Verna studied her plain features and sallow skin — nothing a little makeup couldn't improve. Funny how some women couldn't be bothered to make the most of what they had naturally. Dull brown hair parted on the side. She looked like a Debbie or a Karen. Dull name, dull hair, Verna reasoned.

The woman turned and caught Verna watching her. She smiled, but it didn't help her appearance. Verna saw the signs. The pallid, lifeless skin said she was some kind of user. Alcohol could do that after a few decades, but drugs would do it sooner, and this woman wasn't that old. Verna hadn't touched any sort of illegal substance since she was a teenager. She'd learned her lesson back then — painfully so. There were better kinds of highs.

"You've got such beautiful hair," the other woman said in a husky alto.

Verna melted a little. Why be unfriendly? She smiled and crinkled her nose. "Thanks," she said breathily, reaching up to her curls. "It's a lot of work."

"I know." The woman listlessly touched her own hair. "Too much work for me, though I've never been blessed in the looks department."

"Oh, sweetie!" Verna exclaimed. "Never say that about yourself. It's just not true." She smiled and crinkled again, as though to prove her sincerity. "You'd be amazed what can be done these days." She took a good hard look at the woman. "Your hair, for instance. I can recommend a good conditioner and cream rinse that does wonders. I mean, just look at me — colour for days, and I still have great shine." She batted her eyelashes. "As for the rest, well, a nip and tuck never hurt a body."

"You mean you …?"

Verna shrugged. "Just a little. To enhance the natural. It never hurts."

The woman looked a little shocked. "I've never really considered surgery. You see, I was — I mean, I *am* — a nurse, and the thought of it … well, it's just not me."

Verna's interest was piqued. She was fascinated by surgery

and anything medical. "A nurse! How exciting. Do you get to sit in on operations?"

The woman shook her head sadly. "Not anymore. I used to work in hospitals. Now I mostly work for private sources. I'm on my way to a new job, in fact. It's a place called Shark Island. I doubt you've heard of it."

The look on Verna's face was pure astonishment. "Why — I'm going to Shark Island, too."

"Are you? How peculiar."

Verna laughed suddenly. "That's amazing. I mean, to think we both ended up in the same compartment. Are you going for the reunion?"

"What reunion?"

"You mean you don't know?" She shrugged. "Oh, it's nothing, really. Just a band getting together again after quite a few years. I'm sort of a … a groupie."

The woman gave her a funny look. For a moment, Verna had an intuition. Then again, it was hard to say, especially with women. *Wouldn't it be ironic*, she thought, *if this woman hit on me? She definitely looks the type.*

Verna shook the thought aside. "But why Shark Island? What are you going to do there?"

"I've been hired as a domestic, to look after the owner and his guests. I'll only be using my medical expertise as required."

"How fun!" Verna's mind retreated to the rumours she'd heard. "Is the island really owned by Bono?"

The woman laughed. "Oh, I don't think so! Who told you that?"

"That's what I've heard. I'm just dying of curiosity. Who hired you? Can you say?" She pressed a hand to her chest. "I'm sorry. It's none of my business, anyway. But surely you must have heard the rumours?"

The woman shook her head. "I hadn't, to be honest. I … I've been out of touch. All I know is I was hired by some rich entrepreneur to work on his island for the summer. The offer came completely out of the blue when I needed it most." She paused and gave Verna a timid smile. "Sorry — that's probably TMI."

What she didn't say was that she'd been only too happy to accept. With her past, jobs weren't easy to come by. And she wasn't about to tell this glamour queen sitting across from her that she'd been incarcerated as a guest of the government for the last eighteen months after borrowing a few painkillers from the hospital she'd worked at. Or that she'd lost her previous job for exactly the same reason. The first time it had been hushed up, but now she'd lost her licence and was no longer eligible to work in medical facilities.

"My name is Sandra," she said.

"Verna," the platinum blonde said enthusiastically, extending her hand.

"Good to meet you," said Sandra.

"Likewise," Verna said, crinkling her nose again. "Well, Sandra. Whoever hired you, I predict it's going to be a thrilling time for us all!"

CHAPTER 4

David Merton left the dining car and made his way along the swaying passageway. Just inside the bar, a dark-haired woman caught his eye. Her pink, V-neck sweater showed off her cleavage. A plaid skirt and high-heeled boots completed the outfit. She was a cougar, but David didn't mind them a little older. And this one obviously took care of herself.

He glanced around. All the other booths were occupied.

"This seat taken?" he asked, trying not to be thrown off balance by the train's sudden movements.

The woman looked up, taking in the man with the salt-and-pepper hair, trim body, and muscular arms.

"Why, yes it is." She flashed an inviting smile. "By you, I think."

David laughed and sat across from her. "Thank you."

"Don't mention it. I'm Janice, by the way."

"Good to meet you, Janice. I'm David."

"A pleasure."

David took another look at her face. For a moment, she reminded him of someone else. Someone he hadn't thought of in years. The past vanished as the woman's smile faded.

A waiter came by balancing a tray. David ordered a Coors Light. Janice asked for a refill on her rum and Coke. Small talk ensued. The weather was mentioned.

Their drinks arrived. Janice picked up her glass and sipped.

"So what brings you to Washington, David?" she asked, unwrapping a stick of gum and inserting it lengthwise into her mouth.

David smiled. He preferred to be asked instead of bringing up the topic himself. Not that he was overly proud of what he did. It just seemed less like bragging. When he mentioned what he did, people usually assumed he was rich, though that was far from the truth.

"Real estate. I'm a broker. I'm here to assess an island off the coast. Apparently I've got what it takes to sell offshore property."

An interested look. "And what is that, if I may ask?"

"A big client list." He winked.

For a moment, he stopped to wonder yet again why the owner had requested him personally. He didn't have much of a track record, getting by mostly on small apartment rentals and bungalow sales in the suburbs. Who would ever think him qualified to sell an offshore island — particularly one rumoured to have been the site of highly suspect government experiments? Not that the owner had told him anything about it — he'd done his own investigating before accepting the invitation. But no matter. The letter said he'd come highly recommended. That was good enough for him. In his business, referrals were everything.

Selling real estate wasn't the worst thing in the world, though there was a time when he'd been a high-flying moneymaker who got his kicks selling tricks of a very different kind. But he'd lost his claim in the sweepstakes of life. Or rather, his claim had been tossed aside when he took the fall. He'd been compensated, of course, but those days were definitely over. If he knew what was good for him — and he thought he did — he would stay on the straight and narrow, making the odd sale and picking up over-the-hill sweethearts like this one. Strange how she reminded him of that other girl he hadn't seen in nearly twenty years.

"What's that funny look for?" Janice asked.

David shook his head. "Nothing. You just reminded me of someone."

"Someone good?" She licked her lips and sat back in her seat to watch him. "Or someone bad?"

He smiled. "Good. Sort of. Though it ended badly."

She picked up her glass and raised it in a toast. "Story of my life," she said. "Drink up."

David took a swig of beer and set his bottle down. "What did you say you were doing in Washington?"

"I didn't." She raised her chin and looked at him smugly, exactly the way Sarah used to. "I'm here for a reunion," she said. "Some old friends I haven't seen in a while. Quite a while, in fact."

He held up his bottle. They clinked. "Here's to old friends," he said. "And a few new ones."

Two booths over, a white-haired man turned at the sound of their voices. His clear blue eyes moved over the crowd. The word "reunion" had caught his ear, but the piped-in muzak swelled and drowned out the rest of their conversation.

Crispin LaFey, world-renowned music critic, was on his way to a reunion, too. He was about to witness the return of the Ladykillers after more than fifteen years. Though for Crispin it would be a metaphoric witnessing, of course, since he was legally blind.

The get-together was expected to be an historic event. Still, Crispin wondered whether they would live up to their reputation as one of the most badly behaved groups of all time. Once an anarchic thrash band of the loudest, most garrulous sort, the Ladykillers' reputation had rested as much on their off-stage antics as anything they could reasonably claim to have created musically. After more than a decade, they managed to produce only three slim recordings, since re-released on CD, two of which Crispin believed stood the test of time — but just barely. The third and final album had been crap. Tellingly, it was their most popular work. A much-anticipated fourth record was never finished, though it was rumoured to be just waiting in the wings for a few finishing touches.

Crispin knew the Ladykillers well. He'd covered them since the early days when they were little more than a garage band from the wrong side of the tracks in Spokane. Long after The Who, long after Hendrix or the Motor City Five, the Ladykillers were known for destruction — and not only in the midst of their sets. Loud, violent, and bad-tempered, at times it seemed annihilation had been their intent more than anything that smacked of music-making.

Back then, of course, you could always chalk it up to artistic excess. Nothing succeeded — or sold — like excess. Then came that unfortunate incident at a CD release party where a young woman died. At the time, she'd seemed like just one more victim of an excessive age. Fingers had been pointed all around. Someone went to jail for it for a few years. But if the truth be told, more than one person had been responsible. Even the critics had to shoulder some of the blame. They'd stroked the band's egos and made them into something far bigger than they deserved. Ultimately, their legend had grown to such an extent that everyone thought they were the only important band around. The second coming of punk rock. And for that, he, Crispin LaFey, had been as much a part of it as anyone.

The music died down as a Carpenters tune came on. Crispin heard the couple talking again. She was asking about the island he was heading for.

"It's called Shark Island," he replied.

For a moment, there was a lull broken only by the shushing of the rails beneath them.

"But that's where I'm going," the woman said, placing a hand on his forearm.

The real-estate agent gave her a knowing smile. "Then let's order another round. We'll have a good time getting to know each other." He looked over his shoulder briefly then turned back to Janice. His voice took on a smooth, practised sound. "I know we haven't known each other long," he said, "but I feel I know you already."

"Is that a fact?"

"Yes, it is. So I'm just wondering — is there any chance you'd like to help me in my bid to become a member-in-good-standing of the Ten Foot High Club?"

She looked at him quizzically. "The what?"

He nodded over his shoulder at the washroom door. His eyebrows arched coyly as the tip of his tongue traced the outline of his lips. "The Ten Foot High Club. Seeing how this is a train and not a plane …"

She sat back in her seat and shook her head. "Brother, you are forward."

"Never hurts to ask," he said, taking another pull on his beer.

She smiled. "And sometimes you end up getting what you ask for." She picked up her purse. "Give me thirty seconds. Then follow me."

He watched in the mirror as she headed over to the washroom, unlatched the door, and let herself in.

CHAPTER 5

The limo swerved and came to a stop at the side of the road. An aging rocker, tall and thin in peg-leg pants, sleeveless T-shirt, and black leather vest, got out of the driver's seat and looked at the back tire on the passenger side.

"It's fine!" he shouted to the pair inside, a little louder than necessary.

The rear window rolled down. Clouds of cigarette smoke emerged. A Japanese woman with ragged purple hair and too much eyeliner squinted at him. *She looks like an Asian vampire*, he thought. *Neurotic bitch.* And still as big a pain as ever.

"Check it again, Pete. I don't want to die in this cock-sucking hellhole. Where the fuck are we, anyway?"

Pete made a show of kicking the tire. "It's fine, Sami Lee." Now that he'd started, he would have to go round to all four tires, kicking them one at a time. *Always complete,* the Voice reminded him.

"We're almost there," Pete said, trying not to glare at the woman sitting in the back seat next to Max Hardcore.

Max was the one Pete really worried about. Max with his thinning hair and his middle-aged paunch. He was still bad news, like the number thirteen or a black cat on Halloween. Max was the guy Pete didn't want to offend. If they were going to pull off this reunion gig, he'd have to stay on Max's good side. Hell, they'd all have to stay on Max's good side. Not that Max had a good side. This was one hellbent bad boy. A vicious, drug-addled twat. It was a wonder Kent died of an overdose rather than Max.

Crap, Pete thought. *An entire week on an island with Max and Spike and Sami Lee.* Was there a worse hell he could think of? Not likely, but this was probably the last chance any of them would have to revive their careers. And if anybody needed it, it was Pete Doghouse, né Peter Harrison, from Spokane, Washington. Of all the losers from the Lilac City's gutters, Pete was the least likely to have made it. If he hadn't clung to the ragged coattails of Max and Spike as they battled their way up the punk-rock ladder, he might never have got out. For all the good it did him, though, it almost seemed he'd never left. He'd spent the last decade working in a factory warehouse just to make ends meet.

At work, no one cared that he used to be Pete Doghouse, bassist for the legendary Ladykillers. No one would be impressed if he told them he'd met Joe Strummer or traded dirty jokes with Johnny Rotten. So he didn't tell them. They didn't need to know who he was. Every once in a while, some-one with a keen eye and a good memory asked if he was Pete Doghouse or if he might be related to Pete Doghouse, or even if he knew that he looked a little like Pete Doghouse, but he always denied it. To his fellow workers, he was just another down-and-out Joe who lifted boxes for a living and drank bad beer in dirty pubs after-hours.

He also didn't tell them about the Voice that told him to touch each box twice or crack his knuckles and pat that one three times on the top and another one on the bottom before piling them up in a corner and continuing with his work. They would only have laughed. And Pete Doghouse hated being laughed at. Worse, he could never have explained why he felt he had to do everything the Voice told him. So Pete kept to himself as best he could. He didn't have much of an urge to talk anyway. No sense in reliving past glories.

It was hard now for Pete to believe some of the things he'd seen and done in his time, but the heyday had ended. After the band broke up, he'd faded into the woodwork, like so many other out-of-work musicians from back then. He couldn't even get studio work. Not surprising, since he wasn't much of a musician. No one noticed for years that they could barely play a note, because most of their gigs had been such noisy bash-ups. There'd always been musicians to fix the mess they made of their early records. Max used to joke that he knew only three chords on his guitar. That was close to the truth, but it didn't seem like a joke now.

Pete peered into the car. Sami Lee had crawled onto Max's lap and was giving him little pecks on the cheek. If she didn't keep her mouth shut, Pete thought, he might do something he'd regret. It was bad enough that he had to book time off work to come out here, making some lame excuse about a dying mother-in-law. Then, once they'd decided to drive up together, Sami Lee insisted on going by limo. With her chain-smoking and constant carping, it had been pure torture. Worst of all, Pete had been the one to put the car on his credit card. How the hell did she expect him to pay for it? She probably hadn't thought about that. Max spoiled her, so it wouldn't occur to her that someone had to pay the fucking piper. *Bitch!*

As he stood there fuming, a red Saab zoomed over the crest of the hill and headed straight for them. Pete had just enough time to leap to the shoulder as the car went roaring by. He caught a glimpse of an over-dressed business-type with dark skin sitting behind the wheel. The man barely glanced at Pete as he raced past.

"Fucking asshole!" Pete screamed, shaking his fist as the car disappeared in the distance.

He heard laughter coming from the backseat.

"What are you laughing at?" Pete demanded of the pair huddled together and smirking at him through the window.

"You, you fucking piece of shit," Max said. "Get back in the car. We're gonna miss the boat."

Pete got back in and glared at the couple in the rear-view mirror. They'd already stopped paying attention to him. He checked his image: the pale face, as though he'd grown up under a rock; the now-permanent dark circles under his eyes; and the dry, stringy hair. What a fucking mess. The factory was killing him. Clearly, he spent too much time indoors.

Sami Lee's giggles reached him from the back seat. He looked back to see her smirking.

"Get going, man," Max commanded.

Pete ran a hand through his hair and sighed. *Gotta keep my cool*, he reminded himself. *These two are trouble enough without getting on their bad side*. He turned the key and eased the car back onto the road.

"Remind me again why we're doing this?" he said over his shoulder.

He heard a grunt.

"Money. What the fuck do you think?" Max said.

"You sure you and Spike will be able to get along after all this time?" Pete asked, wondering if that was possible. They'd been inseparable in the early days, like some sort of freakish science-fiction twins. Since the breakup, as far as anyone knew, they hadn't spoken a word to one another.

"Harvey says he's into it," Max replied with a bored shrug. "If that cunt can do it, so can I."

A train sped past them on the left. They held pace with it for a while before it veered off into the hills. They might have outraced it, but Pete had to stop the car every time he saw an Arby's. He didn't know why; the Voice just told him to stop. *Pee time*, he'd say, to groans from the back seat. Or, *Got something in my eye. Won't be a minute.* How else to explain you're under the control of a voice in your head? Then he'd go in, take a breath, and wash his hands in excessively hot water before returning. He didn't know why he had to do it, but if he didn't follow the Voice's commands the tension became unbearable. By now, he knew it was easier to submit.

An hour later they arrived at a small fishing village — mostly locals and a few tourists in town for the season. The car windows rolled down as the three occupants looked around. Sami Lee hated small towns. Small towns, she knew, tended to breed small minds. Anyone different was looked on as an outcast. They were either feared or scorned and sometimes both. Her mother had lived through Second World War Japan — she remembered Hiroshima — so Sami Lee knew humans could adapt. If she had to, she could survive worse. In some ways, punk rock had been kind of an atomic blast.

Pete stopped the car to ask for directions to the boat landing. A woman with a small boy looked the car over. The kid's face was shiny with wonder. *Probably never saw a limo before*, Pete thought.

The woman smiled when he greeted her, but her expression darkened at the mention of Shark Island.

"The wharf's down past Pacific Ave," she told him, pointing out a few clapboard houses up ahead.

"Uncle Mark nearly died on Shark Island," said the boy, his face alive with this colourful bit of news.

"Is that so now?" Max said to the boy through his open window. "What did he nearly die of?"

"Experiments," the boy said, both solemn and proud to impart such important facts.

Max looked at the boy's mother.

An anxious look crossed her face. "My brother-in-law was helping with the construction on the island last year. They said it was just ordinary construction, but I don't know. He's all right now, but he got some bad burns on him when it happened. It was some secret government operation, is what we think."

Conspiracy theory bullshit, Max thought. He nodded. "You know, I wouldn't be surprised if it was aliens behind it. Happens all the time," he said, as the window rolled up and the car moved on.

By the time they reached the dock, a small crowd had gathered. *Fans*, Pete thought with a hint of excitement he hadn't felt since the old days. *They've heard about the reunion*. But in fact, it was just a group of fisherman come to look at an old rig they were thinking of rejuvenating. No one paid much attention to the trio of rock 'n' roll misfits passing by as if they were looking for a costume party that had ended twenty years earlier.

Then Pete saw the red Saab off to one side. He didn't have to guess it was the same car that nearly knocked him off the road earlier. And there, standing next to the Saab, was the man who'd barely glanced at him as he raced past.

The guy was watching them with a cocky expression. Pete thought of saying something to wipe the smirk from his face. In the old days, with Spike and Max and Kent to back him up, he would have done just that. These days he was more cautious. You never knew what son of a bitch might be carrying a knife.

He was saved any further aggro when a big man in a lumber jacket came toward them. He could have been ex-navy or a gym trainer a little past his prime.

"Are you for Shark Island?" the man asked, looking them over.

"That's us," Max said. "I'm Max. This is Sami Lee and Pete."

"Edwards," the man said, holding out a hand. "I'm here to take you over in the boat."

They all shook hands.

Max looked down at the bags. Edwards picked them up without a word and hoisted them over his shoulder.

"Are you a Rain City native?" Max asked.

Edwards gave him a queer look. "You mean a Seattleite?"

"Yeah, that. Are you?"

"No. Just a Spokane boy off his turf."

"You don't say," Max said. "Us, too."

Just then the Saab driver came up to them. "Are you heading for Shark Island?" he asked.

"Yes," Edwards said.

"I'll be going with you then," he replied. He looked at Max. "Hello, Max."

Max gave him a flinty-eyed assessment. Pete knew that look. If he wanted to, Max could take you out with a glance. If he decided in your favour, though, you were treated like a member of the in crowd.

"Who the fuck are you?" Max grunted

"I'm your lawyer," the man said with a wink. "I've been hired to make sure you get what's coming to you."

Max's features hardened. "And what might that be?"

"A fair deal — this time around, at least."

Max nodded gruffly. "What makes you think I need a lawyer to get a fair deal?"

"Believe me, Max — you're going to want my advice before you sign any of those offers they're about to throw at you. You can't trust the record companies as far as you can throw them, which isn't far."

"Record companies?"

"They didn't tell you?"

Max shook his head. It was the first he'd heard of a record deal.

The man gave him a shrewd look. "I'm talking about *Endgame*, Max. They want you and Spike and Pete here" — he glanced over at Pete — "to finish it. If you want to, that is. No one tells the great Max Hardcore what to do. Least of all me. I'm just here to give you my professional advice." He paused. "It worked for you once before."

Max glanced at Pete and Sami Lee, but said nothing.

"You don't remember me, do you?" the man asked.

Max squinted hard and gave him a good look. In fact, he did look familiar, though he couldn't have said why.

"Think back, Max. Twenty years back."

All three of them looked at the guy again.

"What did you say your name was?" Pete said.

"Noni Embrem."

"No shit! Fuck — I hardly recognized you, man!" Max said, grabbing Noni's hand and pumping it enthusiastically.

Pete stared at Noni. He felt unsettled by this turn of events. Noni Embrem had been a brilliant young civil rights lawyer when Harvey hired him to defend the band against manslaughter charges laid when a fan died of a drug overdose after one of their parties. At the time, everything seemed to be against them. Everyone predicted the band would go down, but Noni Embrem's decisive arguing prevailed. The crime had been pinned on the drug dealer who supplied the party favours that night. The group was exonerated.

"So you're joining us on the island?" Pete asked.

Noni smiled. "Harvey hired me to protect the band's interests, Pete. And that's exactly what I intend to do."

Max shook his head. "Fucking Harvey. Does he really think we're going to trust him again?"

"No — he doesn't. In fact, technically this has nothing to do with Harvey. He'll get his cut for bringing you back to the record companies, but I'll be the one to advise you on what terms you should accept from them."

Max grunted. Sami Lee wrapped her arm around his waist. Pete waited and watched. The Voice had nothing to say.

"So where are the others?" Noni asked, looking around. "I can't wait to see them again."

"Gone on ahead in the first trip," Edwards said. "I took them all over half an hour ago. I just got back when you arrived."

He looked up at the sky. Dark clouds were moving in on the open blue.

"We'd better get started. There's a major storm expected to hit the coast later in the day."

"So Spike's really here," Max said, staring out across the water where he could see the outline of an island jutting up in the distance. "Then let the games begin. And may the worst man win."

CHAPTER 6

The ride to the island seemed to take forever. The waves grew in size, steadily rocking the boat the farther out into open water they got. Halfway across, Noni Embrem surreptitiously threw up over the side. He turned and apologized to the others for his seasickness. Sami Lee glanced over, a cigarette stuck in the corner of her mouth, then looked away again. Edwards watched Noni with concern, but said nothing. He had his hands full steering the boat. Clearly, the storm was not far off. Rough water might not be the worst of it unless he was vigilant. Pete began to feel queasy, too. His fingers kept up a steady thrumming on the gunnels. The Voice warned him it would help keep them afloat till they reached solid ground again. Of course his rational mind didn't really believe this, but he was unable to resist. The fear was too strong.

The distant blur that was Shark Island grew in size and intensified as they approached. It seemed to rise out of the ocean to meet them. The island wasn't large — a little longer and wider than a football field — but up close it was foreboding. There appeared to be nothing welcoming about it. Anyone approaching would be put off by the sheer verticality of the dark cliffs that rose some twenty or thirty feet at the waterline. The trees, mainly hemlock and red cedar, grew densest around the edges, forming a barricade. The entire island seemed designed for isolation, as though it resented scrutiny. It wasn't until they rounded the point that they saw a cove facing away from the mainland, the only place where a boat could safely dock and allow passengers to disembark.

The autumn sky had turned grey overhead. The wind, barely noticeable earlier, blew harder as they approached. It carried a chill warning that winter was not far off. Sami Lee turned to look back. The mainland was just a smudge on the horizon, as though someone had been scribbling an outline with a dull pencil before erasing it.

The boat slid onto the sandy bottom of the cove. Edwards leapt out and quickly tied it to the dock beside a wooden boathouse. He turned and offered his hand to Sami Lee. As she reached for it, the boat shifted and she momentarily lost her balance.

She spat her cigarette in the water and glared at him. "Watch it! Are you trying to kill me?"

He shot her a look, but held his tongue. "Sorry. Just a bit rocky at the moment."

Pete made it off the boat without incident. Noni leapt nimbly ashore, his face a picture of relief. Max stepped out of his own accord, balancing his bulky mass as he stretched a foot to dry land. Once on solid ground, they all stopped and looked around. An impressive piece of modern architecture rose three stories ahead of them, dwarfing the trees around it. The severe planes and angles of its cubist design seemed imposing and strange on the deserted piece of rock.

"That's something," Noni said, staring at the house. "Someone has a great sense of style."

"And money," Max grunted.

"Piece of shit," said Sami Lee.

Edwards unloaded their bags and started up the path. The others followed in single file — Noni and Pete walking in front,

Max and Sami Lee behind — picking their way along the path. The house lay dead ahead. As they approached, Pete had the distinct impression it was waiting for them, though he couldn't say why. Maybe it was just from knowing Spike was already inside waiting to come face to face with his former partner, and archrival, Max Hardcore. He was dreading the moment as much as he anticipated it. But there was something else. Something not quite tangible. It hung in the air around them, watching their approach. It almost seemed to be judging them.

The door opened as they climbed the stairs to the front porch. Spike stood there, looking pretty much the same as he had fifteen years earlier. Still skinny as a rake, Pete noted. His hair was a ratty mop with hints of green, not unlike the Joker in Batman, the angry scowl on his face only slightly more entrenched.

Spike stared at them as though he might gun them all down if he had a weapon. A grin broke out on his face. "Maxie! You old fucker. You got fat!"

There was a moment's hesitation before Max Hardcore walked up to Spike, glared in his face, and, without warning, embraced his former partner.

"And you, you cocksucker. You still look like a heroin addict. Fuck you!" Max roared.

Laughter engulfed the pair as they did a jagged little waltz around the porch together before acknowledging the others who had been waiting to see whether the pair would kill or kiss. For a moment, no one knew what to say.

Edwards broke the silence. "I'll take your bags inside. Come in and get settled when you're ready."

He turned and went in.

"I didn't know this motherfucker was invited or I'd never've come," Max said, laughing. "I might have to kill him before he tries to kill me."

"And I can't wait to kick your fucking carcass from one side of the island to the other," Spike replied. "But there'll be plenty of time for that later. Come on inside, all of you, and let's have a drink!"

A ring of curious faces met them in the parlour. The harsh words and edgy tones of Max and Spike's greeting had made it difficult to know exactly what was said in earnest and what in jest. The five people seated there waited hesitantly to see what had just walked in the door.

Verna was first to recover. She approached the newcomers and held out her hand. "Hello, I'm Verna."

Pete stood blinking in the doorway, unable to speak. Max eyed the blonde bombshell standing before them like Venus on the half-shell.

"Well, don't all speak at once, boys," Verna said, hands on hips.

"This is Pete and that's Sami Lee," Max said, pointing. "And I'm Max, of course."

"Of course you are," Verna said. "I know all about you. I'm a true fan."

A cough sounded from the doorway. Heads turned to see Noni Embrem.

"And I'm Noni," he said. "The brown guy."

"He's a fucking asshole lawyer, but he's a good guy, regardless," Max roared as he turned to take in the rest of the room.

"I'm Sandra." A woman came forward wearing a grey skirt and an old sweater. Her face was lined and a stoop seemed to keep her from reaching her full height, but on second glance she looked more worn out than old.

"Good to meet you, Sandra," said Max.

"I'll be doing domestic work. I'm also a qualified nurse, so I'll be taking on occasional duties as health attendant while you're on the island."

Max gave her a cockeyed grin. "Does someone think I'm gonna have a heart attack?"

Sandra shook her head gravely. "Oh, no. It's just a courtesy, really. We're not expecting any medical emergencies."

"Good." Max nodded. *No sense of humour,* he thought. *By the looks of her, I'd say she's probably had it beaten out of her.*

Over in a corner, a hand lifted a glass of beer in greeting. "David here. I'll be your friendly real-estate broker this weekend."

"Are they selling the place out from under us already?" Max looked over at Spike. "Have we made it famous just by setting foot on the ground? Are there hordes of fans waiting to buy the island where Spike Anthrax and Max Hardcore met up after fifteen years?"

"Goddamn right!" Spike crowed.

Another woman stepped forward. Pink V-neck sweater, black dyed hair. Not much of a looker, either, but sexy in her own way.

"Hello, Max," came the sultry voice.

She stood there as Max looked her over.

"Holy shit!" he spat out. "Is that really you, Sarah?"

"Yes, except my name is Janice now."

Over in the corner, the man named David choked on his beer. He hadn't just imagined it when he thought she reminded him of someone else. In fact, she was that someone else. Sarah Wynberg, for fuck's sake. Here she was twenty years later. Obviously she'd changed, too. He could have shit himself. And after they'd just … it was too freaky.

"I recognized her right away," he heard Spike say.

David looked over cautiously, smiling to cover his awkwardness. He couldn't help remembering how she'd pressed against him in the toilet of the train. It was the same Sarah Wynberg all right. Even after all those years, he should have known her. She obviously hadn't recognized him, either. Nor had any of the others. It wasn't surprising. He'd been a skinny runt back then. A little pipsqueak everyone called "Newt." His time in jail had changed that. He might have been a runt going in, but he'd found a constructive way of passing the time: weight training. He was nothing like that pipsqueak kid when he got out. He was a completely new man now and as far as he was concerned he'd stay that way. Not a single one of this bunch was going to know different.

Max laughed and rubbed his hands together like a kid anticipating treats. "Well, it looks like this is gonna be some reunion after all." He glanced around the room. There was one more face he didn't recognize. "I don't believe we've met," he said to the silent white-haired figure seated in the armchair.

The man inclined his head. His blue eyes turned on Max from across the room, but they were eerily vacuous.

"Not in person," the man said, "but we've met in print numerous times."

"Eh? How's that?" Max demanded.

"This is Crispin LaFey, Max," Spike interrupted, lest Max say anything derogatory to such an important writer.

"Crispin LaFey," Max said slowly, as though tasting the syllables. Of course he knew the name. This was possibly the most important rock writer the country had produced, and one of its best-known critics. It was he who had discovered the band. "You wrote the first articles on us all those years ago. I remember." Max stood and held out his hand.

Crispin didn't rise or offer a hand in return. He sat there with a vacant look on his face as Max waited with his arm extended.

"Uh, he's … he can't see," Spike said to Max apologetically, lest Max take offence. "Guy's blind," Spike whispered.

"Blind?" Max said. "Well, fuck me. I never knew. It's an honour to meet you, sir," he said. "I humble myself before your presence." And with that, he did a surprisingly graceful bow to the blind writer.

"It's I who am honoured to take part in this historic event," said Crispin. "I've been looking forward to it for many years."

"So have I," Max said with a deep laugh. "So have I." He looked around the room. "Where is everyone else? Where's Harvey? Where's our so-called new drummer?"

Spike shook his head. "Harvey's not here yet. The drummer's coming with him, apparently. Some big name. It's supposed to be a surprise."

"I'm to pick up Mr. Keill later this afternoon," Edwards said softly. "And, yes, I was told there'd be another gentleman with him then. For now, may I show you to your rooms?"

Edwards picked up Max's and Sami Lee's bags. Noni and Pete took hold of their own luggage.

"You've got the best frickin' view of the water," Spike called out as they turned to go. "Third floor. I'm only on the second. I was going to insist on having that room myself, but then I remembered the lovely lady you'd be coming with" — he turned to Sami Lee, who smiled grimly — "and my better self got the better of me, so to speak. So it's all yours. Enjoy!"

Max and Sami Lee followed Edwards, with Pete and Noni trailing behind. Spike's eyes were glued to his old friend and former partner as he ascended the stairs.

That was almost too easy, Spike told himself. *But I'd better not underestimate Max Hardcore. Not for a second.*

CHAPTER 7

Edwards led the newcomers up two flights of stairs and down a hallway. Each door and adjacent wall panel was a different colour, almost like being in a box of M&Ms. He led Max and Sami Lee to a green door sandwiched between two others, purple and red. Producing a set of keys on a gold ring, Edwards unlocked the room and let them in.

A window faced them directly across the room, offering a panoramic view of the ocean. White caps crested the waves. Sami Lee looked out briefly then turned to Max.

"I wonder what the other rooms are like," she said with a pout.

"Pretty much the same, I'd bet," Max replied.

"I wonder if they are," she said, as though undecided whether to stay.

"This is the room Mr. Keill asked me to put you in," Edwards said apologetically. "The others have all been assigned."

Sami Lee's eyes flashed. "Is that so? You mean we don't have a choice?"

"This one's fine, hon," Max told her. "If you don't like it, we can take it up with Harvey when he gets here."

"Whatever." Sami Lee shrugged. Her hand tugged through her hair, scattering the purple tendrils.

Edwards left Sami Lee and Max alone. Pete and Noni waited for him in the hallway. Checking his list, Edwards directed them to a yellow door and a pink one.

"Quite the colour scheme," Noni joked. "Like modern art."

"In fact, I'm told Mr. Keill had the design based on a famous contemporary painting," Edwards said, "though I'm not sure which work he had in mind."

Noni stood back to regard the hallway. "Probably a Mondrian," he said. "At least, it looks like it could be."

"Listen to Mr. Culture," Max said, from inside the doorway to his room.

"I can afford to sound rich," Noni joked.

The door to Noni's room opened onto a view even more impressive than Max and Sami Lee's. The suite was decorated in a sleek, contemporary style. A two-tone duvet lay across the bed. Pictures adorned the walls. There was nothing of the humble cottage retreat about the place. The influence of an accomplished designer was evident at every turn.

Noni put down his bags and looked around. The place was a top-dollar pad, all right, but he'd seen just as good before. It was a long way from the edge of the jungles in Guyana to the big cities of the world, but one by one they'd all opened their doors to him: Paris, London, Vienna … anywhere he hung his hat was home now. He'd played the colour card when it worked for him, but he quickly dropped the guise when it relegated him to anything with "minority" written on it. Civil rights cases might look impressive on a resume, but they sucked when it came to paying the bills. Noni Embrem didn't do minority. Not anymore.

He glanced out the window. He was a true citizen of the world now, and if he'd bent a few laws and played false with a few abstract concepts like justice to get where he was today … well, it had been more than worth it. If anyone asked, he'd gladly do it all over again, whatever the cost.

Pete's room lay at the far end of the hall overlooking the small cove where they'd landed. The boat sat beached, front end thrust up on shore. In the distance, the water had grown rougher, but inside the cove the waves broke softly against the rocks, as though exhausted by their journey to the island.

On the ride over, Pete had worried the Voice wouldn't like the accommodations he was given, though he knew he might have little say in the matter. But the Voice didn't speak when he entered the room, which was a relief. Pete didn't want to deal with the anxiety it would cause him if the Voice disapproved.

He turned to see Edwards watching him. Was he supposed to tip the man? Apprehension welled up inside him. He fished around in his pocket and drew out a few coins, but Edwards turned them down.

"No need," he said.

Pete put the coins back in his pocket and placed his cellphone on the table beside the bed.

"Dinner will be ready in an hour. Feel free to join us for a drink before that," Edwards said as he turned and left. He quietly conveyed the same message to Noni and Max and Sami Lee as he went back down the hall.

"Are you the bloody cook, too?" Max called out.

"Captain, cook, and chief bottle washer," Edwards replied.

"Mind what you make then," Max told him. "I'm allergic to all forms of shellfish."

"Yes, sir. I've been fully apprised of that. Mr. Keill has asked me to ensure that there's no shellfish on the menu for the entire week. And as Mr. Anthrax's digestion is delicate, I've decided against making any spicy dishes."

"What's that? Spike's gone all delicate on us?" Max laughed.

"So I've been told," Edwards said. "I'll do my best to cater to everyone's appetites, at least as much as I can with the ingredients on hand, of course."

Edwards then headed back downstairs to the kitchen to prepare the evening's meal. He didn't like to admit it, but he was rattled to learn the identities of his guests on the island retreat. No one had told him about a band reunion when he applied for the job. Mr. Keill's highly detailed emails said he would be looking after his guests, but no mention had been made of the Ladykillers.

They were a vile bunch. Not just the band members, but the others, too. The women were even worse. That freakish Asian with too much makeup and the one who looked like a cartoon blonde with her breasts hanging out all over the place. The other one in the V-neck sweater — Sarah or Janice or whatever she called herself — had come onto him before they'd even set foot in the boat. She'd stared at him like a starving animal sighting a meal. He had no use for women like that. Desperate. Edwards preferred a little fight in his women. He didn't want anything so easy. At least Sandra was a modest sort, though anyone could see that all the fight had been beaten out of her.

As for the lawyer, Edwards had no time for the breed. They were all liars and frauds with a licence to kill. They could ruin your life, if you let them. And then there was that blind guy who stared at you till it gave you the creeps. Edwards wasn't so sure he was really blind. There was something about the man's eyes, how they seemed to follow you around the room. The only one he didn't mind was the real-estate guy, David. He seemed all right. How had he got mixed up with this bunch? Probably queer, but they usually weren't a problem. A little flirting never hurt, as long as he didn't have to put out. If Edwards got the chance, he might hint that he'd be looking for a job once this island gig was up. Real-estate agents were always well connected.

One of the reasons he'd moved to the coast was to get away from so-called "civilization." After years of driving taxi in a big city, he wanted as little to do with crowds as possible. These days, he preferred a retreat in the wilds. The coast had been

perfect for that. In fact, he knew that one of the reasons he
got this job was because he'd written on his application that he
enjoyed isolation. The less he had to do with people, the better.
If the truth be told, he was a misanthrope at heart. He had no
use for human scum like the Ladykillers or their entourage.

Edwards turned back to the counter and picked up a
long-handled carving knife. He pressed the blade against the
heel of an onion and pushed down, neatly stripping off the peel.
He made quick work of it and tossed the shreds aside. Cooking
came easily to him. He'd worked as a chef in various hotels in
the evenings after taxi work. It hadn't been a problem for him,
having no social life whatsoever.

As he sliced, an image of the dead girl's face came back
to him. So pretty. Why should someone like that have to die
when scum like the Ladykillers lived? They were users. They
destroyed people. Edwards felt his face heating up as he fumed
and chopped. In less than a minute, the neat white slices were
sizzling in a pan of hot oil.

The smell of cooking drifted into the parlour where Max and
Sami Lee had just come downstairs to find all the other guests
assembled.

Spike looked up. "Good room?"

"Nice." Max looked around, taking in the neatly furnished
quarters. "What's next in this gig?"

"First things first — help yourself to a drink. Or if you prefer
something harder" — Spike motioned to a sideboard where
two small copper bowls sat propped before a mirror — "that's
available, too."

Max looked over at the bowls — one was filled with white powder, the other with an irregular line of spiked joints. "Is that real?"

Sami Lee scooted over and dipped her finger in the powder. She took a sniff and smiled. "Oh, yeah, Maxie. It's real!"

Max nodded grimly. "Harvey must be doing pretty well for himself."

"So it would seem," Spike said. "C'mon — I'll show you around."

He stood and headed for a set of French doors. Max followed. In the drawing room, a guitar, bass, and drum kit waited on a small stage alongside a rank of microphones. On the far side, facing the stage, someone had mounted two high-def video cameras.

Max looked it over critically. He turned to Spike.

"It's all set up, isn't it?"

Spike nodded. "Everything's ready. It's just waiting for us."

Max turned back to the instruments. "Fine, but I'm not playing one fucking note till Harvey gets here. There's no reunion till we talk about what kind of deal we get. And if I don't like it, I'm outta here."

Spike smiled and shrugged. He knew better than to argue. It hadn't worked fifteen years ago. All it had done was break up the band. It was Max's way or the highway. It had always been like that. Some things never changed.

"That's okay, Maxie. We're all in this together," Spike said carefully, making sure to keep any trace of annoyance out of his voice.

Pete stepped into the room. He registered the looks passing between his former and maybe soon-to-be-again band mates. The pair ignored him. He turned his attention to the stage. To his surprise, he saw that someone had gone to the trouble of finding him a burgundy Cobra bass. His had been packed away for years and when he practised now, which was seldom, he used a Toby Deluxe. Beside the Cobra sat a red Telecaster guitar exactly like Max's. And the drum set was a Ludwig, as Kent Stabber's had once been. Someone was clearly anxious to recreate the old days down to a *T*. It left him with a strange feeling, knowing the length they'd gone to complete the setup. The Voice still had nothing to say about it all.

"That's right," Max said gruffly. "I wanna hear it from the fucker's mouth exactly what I'm getting for this. Till then, as far as I'm concerned, this is a fucking martini party. I'll have that drink now."

He turned and headed back to the parlour. Just as he passed Pete, his eye caught the chessboard set up with what appeared to be a game in progress. Max stopped and looked at the scattering of pieces around the board.

"Chess, huh? That's Harvey all over, isn't it?" He gave a harsh laugh. "I guess we just have to sit and wait for him to make his next move."

Count them! the Voice boomed to Pete.

CHAPTER 8

An hour later, the nine guests were seated around the dining room table. Place cards had been set out, indicating where each was to sit. Max and Sami Lee purposely switched places, sitting in Crispin's and Noni's chairs while leaving the wrong cards in front of them.

Noni smiled and made a joke of it when he arrived, taking Sami Lee's place instead. Crispin was directed to Max's seat.

"I've always wondered how it would feel to be the great Max Hardcore," he said, with what might have passed for irony. "Though I'm not convinced I'm any closer to knowing."

"When you find out," Max said. "Let me know."

Verna entered in a low-cut velvet gown, her wrists lined with an assortment of bangles. Janice followed in a blue summer dress, her hair pulled back in a ponytail. They sat across from David and Pete, still dressed in their casual wear. Noting the place card disarrangement, the two women gleefully swapped cards with David and Pete, but keeping the seats originally assigned them.

Both Crispin and Noni had worn dinner jackets. Spike came in last wearing black jeans and T-shirt. He sat at the head of the table looking funereal and authoritarian all at once.

Edwards came out of the kitchen. He noted the seating changes, but said nothing about it.

"Hey, Edwards," Max called out. "What's with the fucking Martha Stewart name cards? Is Harvey afraid we won't know who we are without them?"

Edwards smiled and nodded. "Just one of Mr. Keill's finishing touches. If anybody has any special drink requests, I'll be happy to see what I can do."

Noni looked up. "How special?"

"Sir?" Edwards said.

"I have a request, but I doubt you'd stock it," Noni said.

Edwards cocked his head. "Try me."

"Well, I'm sure you have gin," Noni said. "And a lemon, of course."

Edwards nodded, listening intently.

"But you probably don't carry something called Kina Lillet."

Edwards gave him a curious smile. "In fact, sir, we do have Kina Lillet. Mr. Keill instructed me where to find it in his cellar. There are several bottles."

"That's astonishing," Noni said. "In that case, the recipe is simple: an ounce of gin, stirred with half an ounce each of lemon juice and Kina Lillet."

Edwards gave a curt nod. "I believe that is what is known as a Silver Bullet."

"It is indeed!" Noni looked around at the others. "It really is astonishing, you know. They stopped producing the drink in the 1930s. Something to do with the quinine making it too bitter. I got a few bottles that I bid on at an auction several years ago — very expensive, I can tell you — but I've never known anyone else who had it."

"Harvey always liked the best of the best," Spike said with a knowing look. "Even back when he was pretending to be a prolie like the rest of us."

"Anyone else for a glass?" Edwards asked.

"I'll stick to beer," Max grumbled. "No prissy drinks for me." He looked over at Noni. "No offence there, dude."

Noni nodded at Max. "None taken."

"And for everyone else?" Edwards asked.

"I'll have a glass of red wine," Verna said.

"Oh. That sounds good!" Janice seconded.

"White for me," said David. "Alsatian, if you have any."

"Of course, sir," Edwards assured him. "We have everything you require."

"I'll have the same," Crispin spoke up.

"Soda water for me," Spike said. He saw Max grinning at him and shrugged. "Lousy digestion."

"Beer for me," Pete said.

"I'll have a dirty martini," Sami Lee said, scowling. "On the rocks. Hold the junk."

"One martini, hold the olives," Edwards said. He turned back to the kitchen and soon returned with a tray of assorted drinks. He handed Noni a martini glass. Noni sipped it then sat back and sighed contentedly.

"Perfect," he said. "Absolutely perfect!"

"Now that drink requests have been taken care of," Crispin began, "I, too, have a small request."

The others turned to face him where he sat with both hands on a small portable recording device.

"As we are all aware, this is an historic occasion. I would like to beg your indulgence in allowing me to tape the sessions while we are on the island. It would greatly help in my task of documenting everything if I might be allowed to make a recording of all our conversations — well, perhaps not all, but nearly all that goes on here this weekend."

Faces turned to regard one another around the table. Spike spoke up first.

"I don't think anyone has any objections, Crispin," he said.

"It's all right with me," Max seconded.

"Most kind of you," Crispin said. "I thank you all, as will

posterity one day." And with that, he proceeded to turn on the recorder sitting before him.

As though self-conscious at being recorded, everyone began to speak animatedly. Verna asked if anyone else had heard the rumours about Bono owning the island.

"I heard it was Madonna," Janice piped up.

Max laughed his harsh laugh. "And all the fucking villagers think it's some crazy place for government experiments." He made a face. "Whoo!"

"Well, whoever owns it, I hope they show up soon," Spike cried. "They're gonna miss a damned good party!"

Pete sat and listened to them in silence. The Voice said nothing.

Enticing smells wafted in from the kitchen. Sandra emerged wearing an apron and pushing a cart laden with food. She set the dishes on the table one at a time, removing the covers to reveal an assortment of beef, chicken, veal, and vegetables. Edwards was indeed a capable chef and had turned out a veritable feast in short order.

The guests were busy passing plates and helping themselves when Noni stood and raised his glass.

"Now that we're all together, I'd like to make a toast to the reason we're here today," he said, looking at Spike, Max, and Pete in turn.

Glasses were raised as murmurs of assent went around the room.

"While we've got a bit of work ahead of us," Noni continued, "I intend to do my very best to get you guys whatever you want by way of an agreement from the recording companies before we leave this island. Here's to a very successful reunion of the Ladykillers!"

"Hear! Hear!" cried Spike, as they all drank.

"All I can say," Max said, "is I'm glad it's you. You worked your magic for us last time and I have no doubt you'll do it again this time."

Max turned to the others.

"This bastard got us out of one of the trickiest situations I've ever been in," he continued. "I was sure we were headed for jail, but Noni convinced someone else to take the dive when we thought we were done for. Did you have to bribe the guy much?"

Noni looked uncomfortable for a moment then laughed. "I can't reveal any trade secrets," he said. "And I can only say this in confidence, meaning none of you can pass it along to anyone else." Here he gave a stern look over at Crispin LaFey and his recording device, though the glance went unnoticed by the critic. "And that goes for posterity, Crispin," Noni said.

"What does?" Crispin said with a start.

"What I'm about to say," Noni replied. "Which is that I merely brokered a deal with another party to plead no contest to the charges. I believe a sum of money may have been mentioned at the time. In fact, I was just following orders from Harvey Keill when I passed an envelope on to a certain party right before the trial. A happy ending was ordered and a happy ending was produced. That's all I can say about the incident."

David's eyes were fixed on Noni. He watched the lawyer with a malevolent expression. At that moment, Edwards entered with a fresh bottle of wine.

"Cheers to the chef! The food is excellent," Verna called out.

"Thank you," Edwards said, giving an ironic bow to the room.

"Speaking of happy endings, where is the man of the hour?" Max asked. "When is Harvey coming?"

"I'm waiting for Mr. Keill to let me know when to take the boat across to pick him up." Edwards glanced out the window where the wind blew heavily through the trees. "In fact, I'd expected to hear from him by now. I hope he calls soon. It'll be tricky getting across once the storm hits."

"When you hear from him, tell the fucker we're all waiting for him," Max growled.

"Will do." Edwards smiled politely and ducked back inside the kitchen.

At that moment, a wasp buzzed around the room before landing on the table close to Verna. She shrank in horror.

"Please kill it!" she said, shivering. "I'm deathly allergic to those things."

David reached over and crushed the insect with the bottom of a glass. Eyes were averted from the sticky yellow and black mess left on the table as he wiped it off with a napkin.

Verna looked at him gratefully. "My hero!"

"Any time at all, ma'am," he replied in a southern drawl.

Verna looked around the room and sighed. "I certainly hope there are no more of these things inside. I brought my EpiPen, but I'd hate to have to use it. I've cheated death so many times already, I can't tell you."

The eating resumed. Max took stock of everyone gathered around the table. "For those of you who don't know, there's more than one celebration taking place this week. Sami Lee and me met twenty years ago this coming Sunday. We decided that coming here was a great way to celebrate our — er — ongoing sinful union."

A chorus of congratulations went around the table. Sami Lee looked gloomily at the others and stubbed out a cigarette, but said nothing.

"In fact," Max continued, "Sami and me met through Sarah."

He raised his bottle to the woman in blue at the far end of the table.

"It's Janice now, Max," she corrected in a bright voice. "It was at that party, wasn't it?"

Max scowled at her. "What party would that be, Janice?"

"The party we all wished we hadn't been at," Janice replied. "*That* party."

"Yes, it was, now that you mention it," Max said in a menacing tone.

Glances caught and held briefly around the table. *That* party. This was in-crowd material, though most of the group knew what she was referring to. The table lapsed into silence again.

After a moment, Spike turned to the critic. "Crispin, my friend — what magazine are you representing here?"

Crispin turned upon hearing his name. "Actually, I'm here as a freelance writer," he said. "Once I've finished the piece, I'll sell it to the highest bidder. Perhaps *Spin* or *Rolling Stone*, though that remains to be seen, of course."

Max looked up. "You weren't assigned to cover us by a particular publication?"

Crispin shook his head, his mouth set. "No, I'm afraid not. Most magazines don't have full-time staff writers any more. In any case, I want to keep strict control of the material. In fact, I'm really here because I've been writing a comprehensive history of punk rock. I've already got a publisher lined up. You see, I feel this reunion could turn out to be an important chapter in that history. This could be the beginning of a more generalized revival of punk music around the globe."

Max brightened. "Really? Well, we are honoured again. Glad to hear it."

"Truly, I am the one who is honoured," Crispin replied.

"And in that case," Max said, "I'd be happy to tell you a few of my war stories from back then. We met Rotten and few of the others, so there's a lot of dirt to be dished. Maybe later tonight we'll crack open a few cold ones and chat."

"I'd be delighted," said Crispin. "I love authenticity. Isn't that why we're all here?"

"Absolutely." Max looked over at Verna. "What about you, hon? Apart from our real-estate man, Davie" — he nodded in David's direction — "and the hired help, Sandy and Eddie, we know just about everybody else here. How did you come to be a part of this little event?"

Verna smiled broadly, her eyes sparkling. "I won the *Noise* contest that was held last month. Someone phoned me up a few days ago and said my name had been selected from thousands of entrants. I've been a Ladykillers fan forever, so it was an absolute thrill to be chosen."

"Lucky you," Max said.

Verna beamed. "Absolutely!"

"Why, I won the same contest!" Janice blurted out. "That's how I got to be here. Someone phoned me last week."

"Two big winners," Spike chimed in. "Quite a coincidence."

"The only things is …" Janice paused.

"What's that?" Spike asked.

She gave a little giggle. "Well, I don't remember entering any contest. Of course, I wasn't about to turn it down when they called."

"Double lucky then," Spike said with a laugh.

Sandra cleared away some dishes while Edwards replenished the drinks. A faint buzzing could be heard. He pulled out his BlackBerry and glanced at it then looked up with a puzzled expression.

"I'm sorry to tell you that Mr. Keill has been delayed. I've just received a text message from him."

"Well, does he say when he's coming?" Max demanded. "He knows we can't do anything without him here. This is his game."

Edwards scrolled through the message and looked up. "Mr. Keill says he hopes to be here first thing in the morning. In the meantime, he urges you all to make yourselves at home and get as comfortable as you can." The wind gave a mournful howl overhead at that moment. It suddenly died again as though it had changed its mind. Edwards glanced at the window with a doubtful look, then brightened as he continued to refill the empty glasses. "In the meantime, if there's anything you need, just let me know. I'll do my best to get it for you."

He turned and went back to the kitchen.

Max's fist hit the table. "Well, isn't that just fucking great? Harvey throws this little bash and then can't be bothered to show up."

Sami Lee put a hand on his knee. "He'll be here. You know he wants this as much as we do."

Max nodded gruffly and slumped in his chair.

"Don't worry, Max," Noni told him. "Sami Lee's right. I know Harvey wants this reunion to take place as much as everyone else. He told me so himself, so don't fret."

"I'll murder the fucker if he screws this up," Max growled.

The threat hung in the air. No one spoke for a moment.

"Oh, sweetie, don't even think about it," Verna chimed in, waving her hands and making her bracelets jangle. "Just think of all the preparation he's done already. He's not going to back out now."

David picked up the bottle of white to top up his glass, emptying it in the process. He turned it upside down in the ice bucket. "There goes one dead soldier," he said with a laugh.

For a moment, no one spoke. Harvey's sudden cancellation had hit them all in different ways, though it was clear the party seemed to be on a downward swing, the mood turning glum.

It's too early to start thinking doom and gloom, Spike thought. They would have to get through this weekend and still have the tour to look forward to.

"I'll get another bottle," he said. He stood and headed for the kitchen. As he pushed his way through the door, he saw Sandra standing in front of the fridge. She seemed distant, her thoughts elsewhere. Edwards was nowhere to be seen, though he'd just gone through that way a few minutes earlier.

"Eddie-boy gone out?" Spike asked.

"Oh, I don't …" Sandra looked over with a startled expression. "Sorry. He was just here a minute ago. Do you need him?"

"No worries," Spike said, heading toward her. "More drinks. I'll help myself."

Sandra quickly stepped aside as Spike approached. He caught a whiff of fear. Was she afraid of him? He opened the fridge and looked in. The labels looked expensive, though he knew nothing about wine. He grabbed two bottles closest to the front and let the door slam shut.

"These'll do," he said, heading back to the dining room.

CHAPTER 9

Upstairs, Edwards kept his ear tuned to the goings-on in the dining room. If any of his guests got restless, he might find himself in a very tricky position. Mr. Keill's instructions had been explicit: he was to gather everyone's cellphones without arousing any suspicions whatsoever. He hadn't said why he wanted this done, only that he would square it with them all upon his arrival. A joke of some sort, no doubt. Until then, Edwards knew he had to be careful.

He carried the ring of master keys carefully, trying not to jangle them as he slipped first into one room and then another. He'd managed to get Sandra's cellphone when they first arrived and he got Verna's next when she was busy with her makeup kit. He hadn't been able to find where Spike Anthrax kept his, but then remembered the message said Spike probably wouldn't carry one, not being technologically inclined. He'd let it rest at that, but watched to see where the others put theirs as he showed each of them to their rooms. Most had left them on dressers or bedside tables, but the lawyer, Noni Embrem, had slipped his into the pocket of his jacket. It was going to be difficult getting it from him.

Max Hardcore's red cell was sitting on the dresser beside Sami Lee's purple phone. Pete's was on the table next to his bed, right where Edwards had watched him leave it. The hardest one to locate belonged to the critic, Crispin LaFey. It had been zipped into the lining of his computer bag, but Edwards found it eventually. The laptop's keyboard was in Braille, he noted, slipping the phone into his pocket. So he was truly blind after all.

It was all over in five minutes. By his reckoning, Edwards had every phone on the island except for the lawyer's. He removed the batteries, bagged them all, and slipped downstairs via the back stairwell in time to hear Spike ask Sandra where he was. He heard the fridge open and close again as Spike left the kitchen. If anyone asked, he'd say he was in the bathroom. What could they say to that?

He waited till Sandra was busy gathering dishes in the dining room before pulling out the footstool. He climbed up, pushing the bag into the cupboard over the sink as he'd been instructed, then locking it once he was done. It would be easy enough to find if anyone wanted to search the entire premises, but without batteries the phones were useless. He was about to step back down when he noticed a tin container. Curious, he opened it. It was filled with a vile-smelling white powder. A cleaning agent of some sort, he decided, pushing it farther back. Had it been there earlier? He couldn't recall.

Edwards thought again about his new employer. He wasn't quite sure what to make of this Mr. Keill. Everything had been so specific — the man had made copious notes telling him each guest's food and drink preferences, which rooms to put them in, as well as where to seat them at dinner. He'd been very particular about all of it. In fact, it seemed that nothing had been left to chance except for his arrival. And now Mr. Keill was going to be late.

Edwards hoped the guests wouldn't blame him once they realized their phones were gone. It had all seemed fine at first, but in fact he was no longer sure he liked this job. Despite the excellent pay, it was turning out to be more than he'd bargained for. Though the retainer was generous enough, he had yet to see anything beyond the initial funds that had brought him to the island in the first place.

He got down off the stool and put it away, wiping his hands as Sandra returned bearing a handful of plates. He took them from her and let them slip under the suds in the sink. He hadn't been kidding when he called himself "chief bottle washer."

Sandra went back out to the dining room. The door opened again almost immediately. It was Crispin, the blind man. He appeared confused as he looked directly at Edwards.

"Sir?" Edwards said.

"Excuse me. Is this the way to the washroom?"

"No, sir. It's to your right, down the hall. Third door on the left."

"My apologies. Thank you."

The door closed and Sandra returned a few seconds later.

"Doing all right?" Edwards asked.

"Yes, I guess so," she said. "They seem to be finishing up out there. It's just all a little bit odd, isn't it? I mean, it's strange how the host hasn't arrived in time for his own party."

"Perhaps," Edwards replied with an ironic smile. "You might see if anyone wants any more wine."

"Will do. Though the green-haired one was just in here helping himself."

Edward laughed. Sandra picked up a bottle of red and a bottle of white and went out brandishing one in either hand.

A cell buzzed. For a moment, Edwards was startled as he wondered whose phone he'd missed on his rounds. Then he realized it was his own. It was another text message from Mr. Keill. *Serve dessert*, it said, *then show them the video*.

Easy enough.

Yes, sir. All is well here, he texted back.

Edwards slipped his BlackBerry into his pocket and retrieved nine cellophane-wrapped bowls from the fridge. He'd prepared crème caramel earlier in the day, before the first guests arrived, to allow the pudding time to cool. He slid a knife around the edges, turning them onto dessert plates and arranging them on a tray. He noted with satisfaction how each formed a perfect circle of wobbly custard, like a soft belly, dirtied slightly by the burnt caramel dripping down the edges. Delectable.

He slipped the tray onto a trolley and wheeled it into the dining room. Looking around, he saw that the critic had returned to his seat, but Max and Spike were no longer at their places.

"Who's for dessert?" Edwards asked.

David, the real-estate agent, held up a hand. So did the lawyer, Noni.

"I don't eat sugar," Sami Lee announced reproachfully, as though he might have been trying to poison her.

"I'll pass, too," Verna said. "Got to keep my girlish figure."

"I'll have just a nibble," Janice said with a guilty look, as though the other women's refusal made her out to be a pig.

"I'm afraid I'll have to turn down the offer," Crispin said. "I'm a diabetic. I can't eat anything with sugar."

Edwards held a plate in his direction. "I'm aware of that, sir. And I've made a special portion for you, sweetened naturally without sugar."

He set the plate down in front of the blind critic.

"How considerate," said Crispin. "In that case, I will indulge wholeheartedly."

"Me, too," Pete said. "I don't know about Spike, but you can probably leave one for Max. He eats anything." He cackled in a high, unpleasant laugh, like an old woman with a pack-a-day habit.

"I'll leave one for each," Edwards said, setting them on the table for the absent guests and returning to the kitchen.

Pete looked down at the plate before him. The Voice had been oddly silent all through supper. It hadn't made him count the forks at dinner or worry over whether there was an odd or even number of glasses on the table. Earlier, though, it had made him count the chess pieces in the drawing room.

For some reason, the sight of the board had rattled him. That was when the Voice came booming through: *Count them!* There had been twelve pieces in total — eleven on the board in various states of play, and a final piece sitting off to the side. Pete knew the basics of chess. Harvey had taught him to play when they first met. He was able to recognize that the players were somewhere in the middle game. The endgame was still to come.

But wait, he remembered. That wasn't right. The twelfth piece — a white pawn — hadn't been sitting off to the side of the board at all. It had been *lying* on its side. He'd been tempted to pick it up and set it upright, but the Voice hadn't said to do anything besides count them. Pete knew to do precisely what it said and stop there. If it had more to say, it would tell him. When the Voice went silent, he knew well enough to leave it alone.

Just then a whiff of pot filtered through the open screen door. Spike and Max had helped themselves to the bowl of joints in the parlour. They sat outside on the porch now, just beyond hearing range of the others inside.

"So is this it, then?" Max asked, watching Spike toke. "Where are the hordes of fans Harvey said would be here to prostrate themselves at our feet?"

Clearly disappointed, his bravado had slipped down a notch.

Spike handed him the joint. "Nah — this isn't it," he answered, holding in a lungful of smoke. "This is just the first leg. These are the negotiations. The real deal comes once we get it all down on paper.

"So where's the camera crew?" Max said. "What about this documentary they're supposed to be filming of our reunion? I hate that fucking word: reunion."

"I guess they're coming with Harvey. Harvey said he had everything arranged."

Max took a long toke. "This better not be another one of his loony stunts," he said, exhaling at last.

"It's not — didn't you see the piece in *Noise*?"

"Yeah, I saw it. But I'll kill the fucker if he fucks up again."

Spike snorted. "I plan to kill him anyway. Once the contracts are signed, I mean."

Max scowled. "Right ... that."

Spike took the joint. "Anyway, we know he's not reliable. Remember when he had that idea to give away a free Christmas tree with every copy of our third recording, *Very Bad Dog*?"

Max laughed. "We had the kids lined up for blocks, but he ran out of trees in fifteen minutes ..."

"... and gave the records away for free when he ran out of trees. The idiot!"

"Right — and then he tried to deduct the cost from our percentage. As if it was our idea."

"True enough," Spike agreed. "He was a cunt even back then."

"And wasn't it his idea for that joke track, 'Farting on Demand'? That was just stupid."

"Yeah. That was more of his nonsense. It sounded convincing, though."

A long silence passed between them while the wind stirred overhead. Darkness was descending over the island.

"Penny for?" Spike said, catching Max's pensive look.

"We had our fun. Whatever happens, they can't take that away from us."

"True. But I want more. I don't know about you, but I intend to grow old disgracefully."

Max shrugged. "So maybe we should just cash in on this offer — finish the record and go home."

"I'm all for that. A tour would be nice, but the recording is the real prize as far as I'm concerned. That would prove that we're back on track. It wouldn't hurt to have some royalties coming in too."

Max's eyes lit up. "To be back on the charts again — I'd give anything for that." The scowl returned to his face. "Still, I'm doing nothing without Harvey here. I want to see his blood spilled on that contract before I'll play a fucking note."

"Yeah, me too." Spike looked carefully over at Max. "Still, I've learned to show a little gratitude along the way. How 'bout you?"

Max shrugged and took another toke. "'Course I have! I learned a thing or two over the years. I'm not a total twat." He held onto the smoke before exhaling again. "Just mostly."

Spike sighed. "You know, I always meant to call you. After the breakup, I mean."

"So why didn't you?"

"I stayed pretty pissed about everything for a long time …"

"We were both angry."

"— especially the money thing with Harvey, though we always said we weren't in it for the money. Why didn't you call me?"

"Same reason. Anger. Back then, anyway. It's mostly just a posture now. Something to keep my mind occupied so I don't go crazy."

Spike listened carefully to Max's words, the tone of voice. They were pretty much the same things he'd thought himself over the last few years. But could he trust Max? Not likely.

"So then we're both a couple of twats," Spike said at last.

Max nodded. "Yeah — probably. Though I still think Harvey's the real villain here."

"I agree a hundred percent," Spike said, nodding. He paused. "Do you ever think about …?"

"What?"

Spike shrugged. "You know … that girl."

Max took another toke and turned away. "I try not to. It was a long time ago. What good would it do to think about it now?"

"No remorse then? Nothing?"

Max scowled. "Nah. No regrets. What's the point?"

"You're right." Spike took a final toke and ground the roach out under his feet. He stood. "I gotta piss. I'll see you inside."

Max sat looking out at the water for a few minutes, feeling the smoke loosen him up inside. The truth was, he thought about the girl more than he liked to admit. It was as though she lived inside him now, long after her death. He'd dreamed of her several times over the years and woke in a sweat, trying to get away from her before anybody could pin it on him.

That's just bullshit, he thought. *Fucking ghost story is what it is.*

He was about to go back inside when he heard something crashing in the bushes behind the building. He stood and looked off into the dense brush. Everything lay in deep shadow. The wind stirred in the upper branches like a miniature fury.

He turned the corner and went to investigate.

CHAPTER 10

When Spike got back to the dining room, he found a plate of wobbly custard at his place at the table. He sat with a goofy grin and picked up a spoon.

"What the hell's this? Some kind of goodies for Spike?"

"We know you still like your sticky, sugary treats, Spike. Don't deny it," Janice told him.

"Hell no. I'm not denying it," he said, baring his teeth. "I'm going to gobble it all up, just like the Big Bad Wolf. Grrr!"

Just then David returned and sat. He took a bite of dessert then stopped and looked around the table. "I've lost my cell-phone," he said. "If anybody sees it, it's blue. It's important, so please let me know."

"Do you need to make a call?" Noni asked. "I've got mine right here, if you need it."

"No, no — it's just incoming calls I'm worried about. But thanks."

"Any time."

"Speaking of," Verna said to the table at large. "Are there phones anywhere in this place? There were none in the rooms."

"I noticed that, too," said Spike. "A bit odd for a grand place like this not to have a phone system."

Their eyes swept the room, but there was no trace of a landline.

"It's probably wireless," David said. "A lot of modern places are these days. No fussing about with lines and jacks and whatnot."

Max came in through the side door and stood looking over the gathering. He seemed to be counting heads.

"Are we all here?" he asked.

"I think so," Janice said, glancing around. "Why?"

"Nothing. I just thought I heard someone crashing around in the bushes outside the cabin just now. I looked, but I couldn't see anyone." He shrugged. "No biggie."

"We saved you a treat," Sami Lee told him, holding up the bowl of crème caramel. She ran her hands over the chair beside her. "Sit, honey."

Sandra came through to collect the last of the plates.

"Sandra, honey," Max said, glancing up from a spoonful of pudding. The custard plopped onto the table, though he didn't notice as he put the empty spoon into his mouth. "Do you know if we happen to be alone on the island or are there other cottages somewhere?"

She looked at him with a startled expression. "As far as I know, we're the only ones. I came over this morning with the first load of guests. You'd have to ask Edwards about that."

When Edwards entered a few minutes later, Max put the same question to him.

"I'm fairly sure we're alone here," he said, echoing Sandra. "It's a small island. If there were anybody else around, I think we'd know about it."

Max's face registered curiosity. "How long have you been here?"

Edwards smiled reassuringly. "Since yesterday," he said. "I had a quick look around then, though I haven't been thoroughly over the entire island." He turned to the group. "Mr. Keill has a special treat for you," he announced. "If you'd all like to follow me, Sandra will bring coffee in a moment."

The sound of chair legs scraping the floor filled the air as everyone rose and followed Edwards to the drawing room. Noni paused at the threshold. He was feeling seasick again. Or else the Kina Lillet had been more powerful than he remembered. He waited till his stomach settled and then headed in.

A large screen had been placed in front of the stage, with eleven chairs set up before it. The guests sat and waited while Edwards fiddled with the DVD player.

"So what's all this about?" Max shouted to Edwards's bent figure as he knelt to connect the apparatus.

Edwards looked up. "Actually, I'm not sure. Mr. Keill instructed me to play this DVD after dinner once you'd got comfortable. He was definitely planning on being here for this, because he clearly asked for eleven chairs to be set out and there are only nine of you."

"He sent another text message?"

Edwards shook his head. "Just a note saying to begin the presentation after dessert. Those were his original instructions from the beginning."

He turned to Crispin, who sat in the corner of the room. "I'm sorry you won't be able to see this, sir," he said.

Crispin waved an arm in the air. "Not entirely correct," he said. "Although I am legally blind, I do have minimal vision in my left eye. I can make out shapes and colours, just not very distinctly, I'm afraid. I may have to interrupt once in a while to ask what's happening on the screen."

Just then the screen flickered to life. The title held briefly: *Ladykillers — A Tale of Sordidness and Destruction.* Max cheered. The others laughed and murmured. The word "STARRING" rolled past as the original band members appeared, one by one, followed by their names. There was a moment of silence when the late Kent Stabber showed up, his face captured in a youthful grimace, though he went uncredited.

"Poor bastard," Spike said, shaking his head.

The scene cut to a live performance at a cavernous club. The grinding of Max's electric guitar was undercut by the throbbing of Pete's bass and the late drummer's energetic rhythms. The camera turned to Spike, hands wrapped around a microphone as he snarled out the barely comprehensible lyrics of a song that seemed to be about police and guns and riots.

"That's the Purple Institution," Spike called out over the sound.

"Yeah. It was that Christmas Eve concert we played. God, were we young then," Max said, sounding wistful.

The music pounded on as Sami Lee suddenly appeared along with her name. She looked much the same then, vampirish and seductive, her face hidden beneath garish makeup.

"Beautiful, darling!" Max called out to the screen.

How old is she, anyway? Peter wondered, though he didn't say it out loud. *She must be about a million.*

The song ended as a Ladykillers classic started up: "The Twelve Days of Shagging," sung to the tune of "The Twelve Days of Christmas." Another joke tune Harvey persuaded them to record, though it had caught on quickly in the clubs to everyone's surprise.

Spike sang along to his recorded voice: "On the first day of shagging, my true love gave to me a love song full of hate. On the second day of shagging, my true love gave to me two silver bullets, and a love song full of hate. On the third day of shagging, my true love gave to me …"

The music continued as faces flashed across the screen. Suddenly it was like the old days again: there was Harvey Keill, stoned on something and smiling deliriously, followed by a clip of Crispin LaFey talking to someone off-camera, obviously unaware he being filmed. Their names appeared in dark script beneath the shots.

"It's you, Crispin," Max called out. "Good old Crispin."

"Really?" Crispin seemed a little awestruck to hear this. "What am I doing in this video?"

"Haven't a clue," Spike said. "Still don't know what the point of it all is."

More faces crowded the screen. Next came Janice, a thinner version of her more fleshy counterpart today. The on-screen legend identified her as "Sarah Wynberg." A shot of Noni Embrem followed, standing in a courtroom. His name, too, flashed onscreen."

"Where did that come from?" Noni wondered aloud, without expecting an answer. In fact, he was more worried about containing the contents of his bowels, whose gurgling was becoming a little too insistent to ignore.

A party scene followed. A scrawny young man with a ten-inch Mohawk and safety pins piercing his eyebrows looked out from the screen as he tapped lines of cocaine onto a mirror. The lens zoomed in and he broke into laugher. He spoke to the camera operator, though his words went unrecorded.

"I think he just told us all to fuck off," Janice said, laughing.

David shrank into his seat as the name "Newt Merton" faded in and out on-screen.

"Newt was our supplier," Spike said. "That's the guy who went to prison. I haven't seen him in years. What's going on here?"

But no one had an answer.

The song continued as a much younger-looking Edwards appeared, serious and unsmiling, his thick black hair gelled and combed straight back.

"Hey, Edwards! Isn't that you?" Spike called out.

"I … yes, it is. What in the world …?" Edwards's real-life counterpart watched his former self in mute silence before slumping into one of the empty chairs. He sat there, shaking his head in bafflement as his name, "Jack Edwards" appeared.

Sandra entered the room with a tray of coffee and tea. She'd just begun to pour the first cup when she looked up in time to see her younger self flash across the screen, followed by her name: "Sandra Goodman." She stifled a gasp, dropping the cup and saucer. It shattered on the tiles. With a murmur of dismay, she crouched and began to pick up the broken pieces.

The video continued. Another face flashed on screen — that of an effeminate-looking young man — and the name "Werner Temple." Meanwhile, the song and its lyrics ground on. By the twelfth verse, nearly everyone had joined in:

"On the twelfth day of shagging, my true love gave to me twelve suicides, eleven stabbers stabbing, ten stranglers strangling, nine wasps a-stinging, eight poisoned needles, seven crystals shining, six bombers diving, five tongues of fire, four oceans to drown in, three evil Jujubes, two silver bullets, and a love song full of hate…!"

As they reached the song's climax, the room was abuzz in a roar of combined voices when the word "MURDERERS" appeared briefly then faded out again. On-screen, the band's instruments thrashed but, except for Crispin's, the singing in the room died instantly.

"What the hell is this?" Spike demanded.

A new face suddenly appeared on screen, that of a vivacious, smiling young woman. Sami Lee screamed.

"What the fuck is going on?" Max shouted.

"What's happened?" Crispin asked, startled by the sudden outburst.

"It's that girl!" Pete said, gasping for breath.

"What girl?" Crispin said. "Is someone here?"

The face, friendly and young, faded along with all the others. The words "THE VICTIM" appeared on screen and held a moment before fading out again. A final phrase followed: "ALL THE MURDERERS WERE FOUND GUILTY AND SENTENCED TO DEATH." The song ended and the screen went black.

For a moment there was absolute silence in the room, then everyone started talking at once.

"What is going on here?"

"… who was that?"

"Is this some sick joke?"

"… a ridiculous game."

"Will someone please tell me what the fuck is happening?"

"This is preposterous …"

"… in very bad taste."

"Everyone shut up NOW!"

The final voice was Max's.

The chattering died. Holding the shattered pieces of the cup and saucer, Sandra sank into the last empty chair. The eleven people seated in the room looked at one another in bewilderment.

After a moment, Edwards stood and went to the DVD player. He looked at it as though it might yield some clue to the video they'd just watched. Then he flipped the switch and the screen died. He sat back down, holding his head in his hands.

"Where's Harvey?" Max demanded. "I want an explanation for this!" He turned to Edwards. "Where is your fucking boss?"

Edwards shook his head. "I don't know. He said he was coming. I haven't heard a word from him since he instructed me to start the video."

"Well, when did you last see him?" Max insisted. "Was he in the village on the mainland?"

Edwards looked up with a strained expression. "I don't know. I … I've never met him."

"What?" Max was incredulous. "You mean he hired you without meeting you in person?"

Edwards nodded.

"Why were you in the video?" Spike asked.

"I have no idea," Edwards replied with a stunned look. "That footage was taken at a private party years ago. I didn't know

Harvey Keill then, either. I have no idea how he got hold of it. I just applied last week for a job as a general handyman, cook, and boat driver. The ad was in a local paper that was left in my mailbox. It's the sort of job I've been doing here for the last few years. I sent off a letter with my resumé and got word by phone that I'd been hired and was to report immediately for Shark Island."

"What about you?" Max said to Sandra. "Have you met him?"

The timid-looking woman shook her head fearfully. "Never," she said in a whisper. "I was hired over the phone, too. Someone called to say I'd been recommended."

"Who by?" Max asked.

"I don't know. He never said."

Spike turned to the group. "I think Harvey's playing one of his very bad jokes on us ..."

"It's not a joke if he's accusing us of murder," Janice said in a subdued voice. "That's what I think."

"Well, Harvey can go fuck himself," Max said. "Nobody's accusing anybody of anything. Except for Sandra and Edwards, everybody in that video was someone we used to know back in our party days. All good people. Good fucking people." Here, he looked carefully over the crowd. "And most of those people are in this room right now."

"But not everybody in that film is still alive," Pete told them.

"That's right," Spike said. "Kent's dead. And there were a few others I haven't seen or heard of in years. Like Newt Merton and Werner Temple."

"That little creep Werner," Max said, shaking his head. "God knows I hope never to run into him again. The sight of him makes me sick."

Heads turned at the sound of a chair scraping across the floor. Noni Embrem stood before them, his drink outstretched as though he were about to make another toast. Something about his face said otherwise, however. His mouth hung open and his eyes looked wildly about the room. He seemed to be gasping for breath. He swayed before them, then dropped his glass and fell to the floor with a thud.

Sandra knelt, feeling his neck for a pulse.

"Ice," she said to Edwards. "Get me some ice and wrap it in a towel."

She began to apply pressure on Noni's ribs, pushing down and releasing again, repeating the action. Edwards returned with ice wrapped in a hand towel. Sandra looked up, a stricken expression on her face.

"He's dead," she said.

"What?" Janice looked down at Noni. "How? How can he be dead? He was all right at supper."

Sandra removed her fingers from Noni's neck and sat back. "It must have been a heart attack. It was … very sudden."

"Well, do something! Aren't you a trained nurse?" Sami Lee demanded, her eyes flashing.

Sandra shook her head. "I don't have the proper equipment for this sort of thing. We're not prepared for emergencies. If I had a defibrillator, I might've been able to save him. But there's nothing on the island," she said, with a panicked look. "Really, you've got to believe me. There's nothing I can do."

Edwards knelt and put his hand on her shoulder. "It's all right," he said. "We understand."

"It was that fucking video," Spike said angrily. "That's what caused his heart attack. He'd just been accused of murder …"

He let the statement hang in the air.

"It was awful," Janice said, shaken.

"Harvey will pay for this," Max said, looking around the room.

The others stood there silently, looking everywhere but at the dead man lying on the rug at their feet.

"I suggest we should all think about making it an early night," Edwards said after a moment. "The storm is nearly on us. I'll make some calls. There's nothing more we can do till the morning."

In all the commotion, no one had noticed how the wind had increased outside. They all heard it now.

"I agree with Mr. Edwards," said Sandra, looking around at the others.

There were murmurs of assent around the room as one by one the guests started to drift off, glad to leave the problem in someone else's hands. Crispin, Verna, and David headed upstairs immediately. Sami Lee and Max left next. Janice remained standing in the room with Spike and Pete.

"Do you really think the video caused it?" Janice said.

"It's impossible to say," Edwards told her gently.

"But why would Harvey accuse us all of murder?" She shivered. "He was as much a part of it as anyone —"

Spike gave her a sharp look. Janice broke off.

"Nobody's guilty of murder," Pete said forcefully. "It was an accident. We all agreed —" He, too, left his statement unfinished.

"It's awful," Janice said, looking down at the dead man. "I can't believe he's gone, just like that. I suppose it could happen to any of us, really."

"I used to see it at the hospital," Sandra told her. "You never really get used it, but it happens all the same."

Janice sighed. "I suppose. But I'm far from used to it."

She put a hand to her head. "I'm getting an awful headache. Do you have anything for it?"

Sandra nodded and stood. "Yes," she said. "Come with me. I can fix you up."

The two women went off together.

After they'd gone, Edwards looked at Pete and Spike. "I hate to ask, but would you mind helping me move the body?"

Pete's head hung down on his chest. He was waiting for the

Voice to speak. It had been oddly silent all this time, but something felt imminent.

"Where do you want to put it?" Spike said.

Him, the Voice said at last. It was almost a relief when it finally spoke. The Voice's silence unnerved him almost as much as the things it told him to do.

"Him," Pete corrected.

"Yeah, sure. Him. It. Whatever," Spike said in a subdued tone.

Edwards drew a deep breath. "There are no vacant rooms. For now, we should just bring Mr. Embrem upstairs and put him on his bed." He shook his head. "I doubt there's much chance this will turn out to be a mistake and he'll wake up in the middle of the night, but if he does, I think he'd want to be somewhere comfortable rather than out in the boathouse or somewhere like that."

The three men carried Noni's body up the stairs. They had just placed him on his bed when Max appeared in the doorway watching them.

"Harvey will pay for this," he repeated malevolently then turned and went back into his room.

Downstairs, the Voice said unexpectedly to Pete. For a moment, he looked around to see if anyone else had heard it, but of course no one else ever heard the Voice. He waited a beat then slipped back down to the drawing room.

At first, everything appeared as it had when Noni fell and died. Outside, the wind whined fiercely in the trees and thrashed around the chimney. The storm was on them at last. Pete looked around the room, wondering what the Voice wanted him to see. Then he spotted it. A second chess piece — a black knight — lay on its side next to the white pawn. Ten figures remained upright.

Pete thought about it for a moment and decided he wouldn't say anything about it to anybody else. Not unless the Voice told him to, of course. It might not mean anything to anybody else. Of course, someone could have accidentally knocked against the board in all the confusion after Noni fell. But he didn't think that was what happened. To Pete, it was clearly a sign of something.

Something bad.

CHAPTER 11

Pete stood in the middle of the room staring down at the ivory pieces. How often had he felt like a pawn on the chessboard of life? Even when he'd acted the king, he knew he wasn't one. Still, everyone had taken from him as though he were some kind of monarch with bottomless pockets — first his mother, then later his girlfriends. But when the fame faded and the money dried up shortly after, they'd all left him. It hadn't been him but the money they'd wanted, after all. His mother had gone first, when he could no longer support her drug habit. Rachel went soon after, letting him know just how unnecessary he was: *But you're nobody now, Pete. Why would I stay with you?* At least they were up front about it. He'd never had any real power, not even in the group. It had all been, "Pete, do this," and "Pete, play it like that." No questions asked. He'd been too timid and shy, really, under the armour of being a tough punk. In truth, he had no spine. Without the group, he was nothing.

But that girl, Zerin, she would have been different. He could tell just by talking to her the few times they'd met that she really cared about him. If she'd lived, she might have become the queen to his king, because he knew deep down inside there was a real king underneath it all. A noble, kind king who rewarded the people who were loyal to him. But Zerin died and that was tragic. For that, he blamed all the others, but most especially he blamed Spike. In Pete's mind, it was Spike's fault for inviting her to the party in the first place. And then later for abandoning her. For leaving her on her own where …

He shook his head. He didn't like to think about that, either.

Pete looked over the instruments, thinking back on the times when the band performed together. All had been going well until that stupid party. The Voice hadn't been talking to him yet, otherwise it might have warned him not to get involved. It had also been oddly silent on the question of whether or not to come to the island today. But then he had no choice, had he? He needed this opportunity as much as he needed the money.

Still, the signs weren't good. His thoughts returned to the dead man. Seeing Noni Embrem standing at the dock when they arrived had been a bad sign. He knew it as soon as he recognized Noni as the man in the red Saab that almost ran him down. A very bad sign. And Noni Embrem was a very bad man. Everyone knew what he'd done, but no one was willing to admit it, even now.

He was still standing by the stage when Max and Spike returned. Max came up and put an arm around Pete's shoulders. Together, they stood looking down at the spot where Noni had fallen and died.

"Poor son of a bitch," said Max, with genuine feeling.

Pete eyed him. "Poor son of a bitch, nothing! The man was a slimeball, pure and simple. We all knew it."

Max's mouth fell open. "Hey! Have some respect for the fucking dead. And have some respect for the man who saved your ass from jail once upon a fucking time."

Pete hung his head in silence.

Spike looked at Max. "Pete's right, though. Noni was once a well-respected civil rights lawyer. That all changed when he got us off the murder rap. After that, he began taking on bikers and corporate sleazeballs who'd wiped out pension funds for thousands of employees. And he got them all off, one at a time. It was like we handed him the key to a new world of depravity."

Max glared at him. "Wake up, Spike. What do you think lawyers do for a living?"

Spike shook his head. "Noni didn't need to go in that direction. His reputation was spotless in the beginning. He went from being a minority superhero to a slimeball who would take on any case, no matter how vile, for money. The world hated him, but by then he was rich, so he didn't care."

"Yeah, well — tough. He's dead and we're alive, so don't get hung up on it. And when did you get so lily white? He saved our asses once, so at least be grateful for that."

"True," Spike said softly. "I never liked the way he went about doing it, but it's done and behind us."

"He hung the rap on the bugger who was responsible," Max said in an angry undertone. "Never forget that."

Spike sighed and cast a glance over the stage setup. "So what are we going to do now? I guess once Harvey gets here in the morning this will all be over."

Max eyed him. "Hell, no! We're not turning back now." He stabbed Spike in the chest with a stubby finger. "We are not giving up this opportunity. We're gonna complete that record and we are going back on tour." He turned to Pete. "Right, Pete?"

Pete shrugged. "If you say so, Max."

Max nodded hungrily. "I definitely say so. Ladykillers will ride again." He paused to think for a moment. "Tomorrow we send the women home when they take Noni's body away. Then, when Harvey gets here, we'll put trouble aside and get down to business. Agreed?"

The three men exchanged glances. They all nodded at once.

"Good. I'm gonna have another spliff and then I'm off to bed. Tomorrow's gonna be a busy day."

Max plucked a joint from the bowl in the parlour, then headed upstairs. Passing an open door, he saw Janice pacing the length of the room. Sandra sat on the bed, going through a first aid kit.

"I hope it's not a migraine," Janice was saying. "They have a tendency to strike when I get stressed."

She'd inherited the trait from her mother, Ruth, a chronically worried and unhappy woman who grew up in Holland after the war before moving to the States. She'd passed the whole bag of nervous headaches and fears along to Sarah Wynberg, a.k.a. Janice Sandford, her only daughter. When her mother lay dying, her last request was to be buried in the homeland. They'd all thought she meant Israel, but she was talking about Amsterdam. All that angst. Who could live with it? You didn't grow up the child of Old World Jews and escape the non-stop stories, Janice knew. Better to create your own stories and escape from it all.

Sandra looked up at Janice with a sympathetic expression. "I'd say this certainly qualifies as stressful."

"Stress?" For a moment, Janice thought Sandra had read her mind, but then she remembered she'd mentioned stress a moment before. *My memory's going too*, she thought. *But I'll worry about that later.* "Yes, it's the stress," she agreed.

Sandra continued to look through the kit then dug for something at the bottom. She held up a transparent orange vial with a white top.

"Here," she said, unscrewing the cap. "It's codeine. It should help. You'll sleep well with this."

Her hands quivered a little. Funny how she hadn't noticed the container earlier. Probably a good thing considering her … tendencies.

Janice stopped pacing and looked over at the side table where she already had a vial of sleeping tablets at hand. But the ones Sandra was offering were free. Why not try them?

Sandra shook two tablets into Janice's outstretched hand.

Before she could get the cap back on, she let two more fall into her palm. Quickly, before Janice noticed, she slipped them into her pocket.

Just then there was a sharp knock on the door. Spike's head poked in.

"Everything okay in here?" he asked.

The two women turned to look at him.

"Yes," Janice told him. "I just needed something for a head-ache."

"All right." Spike hesitated. "Sleep tight, then."

When he'd gone, Janice sat beside Sandra on the bed.

"I …"

Sandra watched her with concern. "You can tell me," she said. "Whatever it is, it's safe with me."

"That girl," Janice said. "The one at the end of the video." She shook her head. "She, um, took something at a party in my home. It was ecstasy. She died."

Sandra took her hand and squeezed it.

Janice's gaze was a long way off. "You see, it was … well, the band were having a CD release. We all went back to my house. I guess nobody realized how serious it was at the time, but she died."

The last word came out in a whisper.

Sandra nodded. "It was nobody's fault," she said, in a tone she hoped sounded confident.

Janice shook her head. "It was everybody's fault. All of us. Just like the video said. It was horrible. She lay there quivering for a long time before we even … did anything about it. We were afraid. Afraid of being caught and held responsible if they found out she'd been given ecstasy at the party."

"You couldn't have known," Sandra said soothingly.

"No," Janice said with a harsh laugh. "You're right. I couldn't have known, because I was in bed with the dead girl's date most of that time."

Above them, the storm thrashed about the eaves.

Janice was beginning to relax a little. Tears formed at the corner of her eyes. She sighed and looked up. "Thank you. I feel better having told you."

Sandra smoothed the hair over Janice's brow. She was reminded of a girl she'd known in prison. Crazy Emma. Just friends, of course. Such a pretty face. Not that Janice was pretty, but there was something similar about them. The full lips, the slightly down-turned mouth that hinted at unspoken sorrows. Sandra would like to have kissed those lips — both Emma's and Janice's — though she knew it wouldn't be appropriate. Especially not now, given the circumstances. Maybe tomorrow, in the morning light, she might get up the courage to tell Janice how she felt about women like her. About wanting to soothe all their pains and fears and make them go away forever.

"You should sleep well now. I'd better go see if anybody else needs anything," Sandra said. "I'll see you in the morning."

And then, without thinking, she did what she'd wanted to do for most of her adult life. She leaned in and kissed Janice on the lips. And, to her surprise, Janice returned the kiss.

It was only for a moment, though. Janice broke it off. She smiled wanly and looked into Sandra's eyes. "You're very sweet," she said. "I'd better go to sleep now. I think the pills are starting to work already."

"Yes," Sandra said, smiling down at her as though she'd done no more than tuck a child in under the covers.

"Thank you," Janice said. "For listening to me." She clicked off the bedside lamp.

Sandra went to the threshold and stood staring back into the darkness for a moment. "Sweet dreams," she said, before going out and closing the door behind her.

She continued down the hall, knocking softly on doors where light seeped through under the sill. Crispin called out in answer to her knock, but assured her he was fine and not in need of any sleep medication.

The light was already off under Max and Sami Lee's door. Spike was still awake — she could smell the marijuana. He was fine, he called in answer to her question. The light in Pete's room was off, but she heard him inside muttering to himself. She knocked. After a moment, he opened the door in pyjamas and a ratty-looking T-shirt. His bleary eyes stared straight ahead as if he were looking into another dimension.

"I, uh, was wondering if you needed anything," Sandra said, fighting to hold her gaze steady and wondering why he made her feel so nervous.

"No, I'm okay," he said, nearly shutting the door in her face, as though she were an unwanted salesperson.

Next door, Verna answered Sandra's knock in her nightgown. Her breasts were outlined by the thin material and swelled with each breath. She smiled warmly when asked if she needed anything.

Verna shook her head. "Thanks, sweetie. I'll be fine." Then she reached out impulsively and hugged Sandra. "You sleep tight, too," she said.

Sandra came to David's door last.

"Come in," he called out.

She turned the knob and entered. He lay in bed with his torso exposed, the sheets pulled up to his waist. He gave her a curious look as she hung in the doorway.

"Why don't you come in?" he asked.

"I was just making sure everyone was okay," Sandra told him nervously. "It's been a difficult night. Is there anything you need?"

David ran a hand over his chest. "Like what?"

Sandra felt the repulsion she always felt when men looked at her that way, though it hadn't happened in a while. There had been a few male guards in prison, but now that she'd reached her mid-forties the looks and the offers came less and less often. Still, there were some, like David, who gave her the come-on. And it always brought her back to that day in the ravine after school when Waylon Morphy and the other boys had … but no! She wouldn't think about that.

She held tightly onto the doorknob. "I could give you something to help you sleep," she replied in a sombre tone. "If you want …"

"If you're suggesting medication, I'm all right in that department," he told her. "Company now, that would be nice. If you're up for it."

She felt the grimace taking over her features. "That's not what I meant," she said icily, and left the room.

"No offence," he called after her.

God knows she's not a looker, David told himself. *Anyway, there was no need for her to take it as an insult.*

Sandra returned to the kitchen and began to put everything away for the night. While it might seem heartless to worry about domestic duties after there'd been a death in the next room, she knew it might help her put her mind to rest. She felt in her pocket for the tablets. They were warm and firm to the touch, but she wouldn't take anything just yet.

As she thought back over the events of the evening, her breath quickened. She, too, had been named in the video. Which meant that someone believed she was in some way culpable for that girl's death. How strange, after all these years, to discover that someone knew about her part in the mishap. She'd never met any of the band members before, yet she was clearly implicated in the tragedy along with them. And whoever knew about it was right, of course. While she hadn't done anything intentionally wrong, hers had been one odd part in an unfortunate chain of events that had lead to the girl's death.

She reviewed the case in her mind. After all these years, her memory of that night was still crystal clear, even down to the diagnoses and the treatment prescribed. The girl had taken a bad dose of ecstasy at a party for the band in Janice's house, as she now knew. When they realized the girl was in serious trouble, they'd put her in a taxi and sent her to the hospital. Only there'd been no one to speak for her, and it had taken a long time to figure out what her problem was.

What was clear to the emergency-room workers, once they began to monitor her symptoms, was that she was suffering from arrhythmia, seizures, renal failure, and cardiovascular collapse. This had been followed by pulmonary edema, cerebral bleeding, hepatotoxicity, and cerebral edema. The words were etched on Sandra's brain.

The doctor on call that night had correctly ordered complete blood chemistry evaluations and liver function tests. He'd prescribed benzodiazepines to prevent the seizures, phentolamine for hypertension, beta blockers for tachycardia, dopamine for hypotension, and dantrolene for hyperthermia. Somehow, Sandra had doubled the dose of benzodiazepines.

By the time they realized the mistake, the girl had slipped into a coma. They did what they could to reverse it, but by then it was too late. Nevertheless, it was hard to say what part this had played in the order of events overall. Even if Sandra hadn't been muddled in her thinking — if she hadn't been using that night — and hadn't mixed up the dosage, giving her nearly twice what the doctors ordered, the girl still might not have lived.

Or she might have been left alive but brain dead. That would be the worst thing. In her mind's eye, a curtain lifted momentarily and she saw the faces of all the others she had helped along in similar circumstances. The ones she'd helped out of their dilemmas. She hadn't been able to stand the thought that those women would lie there helpless until they died natural deaths, unaware of the indignities their bodies might suffer at the hands of others. The hands of men. So she'd … helped them. That's what she had done. But the girl at the party — she had been beyond help. Even if the doctors hadn't eventually agreed she was beyond help by the time she reached them — and the courts had later argued the same thing — Sandra had felt it all along. So she had simply helped her in her own way.

Except it had been an accident. She'd administered too much of a prescribed drug. An accident, yes. Like pretty Emma dying. And that sweet Janice upstairs for throwing her party. Because surely it had been an accident of the worst kind for that girl to have come to her party and for the others not to realize what was happening until it was too late.

Sandra tried to put herself in Janice's place. How she must have suffered all these years thinking she'd been to blame for what happened. How Sandra would like to soothe Janice's fears and help her put those terrible memories behind her …

A floorboard creaked and she nearly jumped out of her skin. She whirled to find Edwards watching her.

"I'm sorry," he said. "Didn't mean to startle you."

Sandra reached up a hand to brush her hair behind her ear. "It's all right. I'm just a bit jumpy tonight."

"Understandable."

Edwards was a nice man. At first she'd been worried because his room was right beside hers, the only two people on the ground floor. He hadn't made a pass at her or done anything off-putting, however. Perhaps she could confide in him. But why would she? She was the caregiver here.

"Is there anything I can do for you?" she asked in a calm tone. She suddenly recalled David's response to that question. She didn't want to give Edwards any ideas. "Something to help you sleep, I mean."

Edwards smiled and shook his head. "Thank you, no. It's ten o'clock already. I just came down to close up in here."

He checked the kitchen windows and headed to the back door. It was locked. He turned and looked at her. "I suppose we should both retire," he said.

"Yes," she said.

Her mind was back in prison, the day she'd helped Emma in the pharmacy. Such a beautiful, tormented girl. But she'd died before they really got to know one another. It was a tragedy how everyone she loved ended up dead, Sandra thought. Everyone.

She looked up. Edwards was still standing in the doorway.

"I had another message from Mr. Keill," he said. "He expects to be here in the morning."

This was the first time Sandra had seen him look worried. He turned his head to the sound of the wind outside. It was much stronger now.

"It'll be tricky going over to pick him up if the storm keeps up, but it has to be done," he said.

He stood there watching her a while longer, then turned and left the room.

CHAPTER 12

The wind battered the house all evening long. The rain started a little past midnight. There was no let-up as a bleak and dismal dawn seeped into the sky and filtered across the horizon.

Sandra was up first, at a quarter past seven. As she dressed, she listened for sounds of Edwards stirring in the room next to hers, but there was no sign of life. Like her, he was the silent type who could move about largely unnoticed and unheard. She busied herself in the kitchen making coffee and setting the dining room table before the guests came downstairs. Edwards arrived fifteen minutes later.

"Were you able to reach anyone on the mainland last night?" she asked.

"No, but I left a message. I heard from Mr. Keill. He's handling things on his end. I'm to pick him up at ten." Edwards looked out at the rain lashing the windows. "It looks pretty dicey out there. I'm not looking forward to it."

Sandra's face wore a serious expression. "Maybe you should suggest that he wait till the storm is over."

"I've thought of that," Edwards said. "But it's his show. I suspect he knows what he's doing."

He went back to the kitchen.

Sami Lee and Max arrived in the dining room first. They were followed by David and Crispin. The white-haired critic crept into the room before sitting silently by himself in a corner. *He looks like a garden gnome*, Sami Lee thought. *A creepy little garden gnome.* Though he spoke little, he seemed grateful for the company, unlike the previous evening when he seemed merely to be tolerating the others.

"I've had word from Mr. Keill," Edwards announced as he brought in breakfast. "I'm to take the boat over to the mainland in an hour and pick him and his travel companion up at ten o'clock."

Max took this in with interest. "The new drummer, I suppose. Then I guess he still wants to go on with the plans?"

Edwards looked over. "He didn't say, sir. He sent his profound apologies to us for what's happened. He'll come back over here and get everything sorted out. I understand he's made arrangements for Mr. Embrem's body."

"Is it wise to go out in this weather?" David asked, with a glance at the window. "It's not exactly calm out there."

Edwards cocked his head. "We'll be fine, sir," he said. "Nothing to worry about."

Spike arrived a few minutes later, followed by Verna and Pete. Greetings were exchanged as the guests helped themselves to the meal. Despite the upset of the evening before, their appetites were hearty. The food soon dwindled and all but disappeared.

"We'd better save something for Janice," Verna said, looking around the table. "Has anyone seen her?"

Sami Lee shook her head. "Didn't hear a sound from her room. She's right next door to us."

"I gave her something to help her sleep last night." Sandra said. "She was worried she might be getting a migraine. I'd let her sleep a little longer just to make sure she's fully rested when she wakes up." She looked up just as Edwards returned with more food. "Please go ahead and help yourselves. Mr. Edwards will cook for her when she comes down. The rest of you eat up."

A thought occurred to Max. He looked over at David. "By the way, did you ever find your cellphone?"

David shook his head. "Not yet, though I forgot to look again after all the excitement last night."

"It's funny," Max said. "Because mine's missing, too."

Verna's head whipped around toward him. "So's mine!"

"And mine," Crispin added hesitantly. "Though I may have misplaced it. It could be sitting out right in the open and I might have missed it."

Max turned to Spike and Pete. "How about you two?"

Spike shook his head. "I don't carry a cell. Can't figure out how to operate the damn things."

Pete looked glum. "I didn't check to see if mine was still there, but I think it was right where I left it the last time I looked."

"If you have need of a phone, I can offer you mine," Edwards broke in, hoping to deter their interest in the missing cell-phones at least till his employer arrived. *Let Keill explain it to them*, he thought. After the death last night, it wouldn't seem like much of a joke. If it was a joke.

The clock crept around to nine, but there was still no sound from upstairs.

"I'll go and give Janice a gentle nudge," Verna said. "We don't want her to oversleep."

She left. Sandra went to the kitchen and returned with a fresh pot of coffee a few moments later.

Verna came back down the stairs with a sombre look. "I'm worried," she said. "I knocked several times, but there was no sound in the room and the door's locked." She turned to Edwards. "You have a passkey, don't you?"

"Yes," he said. "I'll get it and we can go up together, if you like."

"I'd feel much better knowing she's all right," Verna said. "Just to be sure."

Edwards went off and returned a moment later with the ring of keys. "Here we go," he said. "Let's see if we can't get her to wake up."

They left together and soon could be heard climbing the stairs. The others turned back to the task of eating and drinking. It wasn't long before Verna returned alone. She looked wildly around the room.

"She's dead!" she said in little more than a whisper.

"What?" Sandra whirled to face her. "How can that be? She was fine last night when I left her."

Verna shook her head and pushed a lock of hair behind her ear. "She's completely cold. I touched her skin."

"Are you sure?" It was David. He looked at her with anxious eyes.

"Go see for yourself if you don't believe me," Verna said.

David stood and left the room.

Crispin spoke in Sandra's direction. "Didn't you say you gave her something to help her sleep? What did you give her?"

Sandra looked panicked. "I … gave her codeine. Just codeine tablets."

"How many?" Crispin asked. "I merely ask because it may have triggered something in her system."

"Two," Sandra replied hoarsely.

It's not possible, she thought. *Last night I kissed Janice, who kissed me back with great tenderness. And now she's dead.*

"Is it possible," the critic went on, "that she had an allergy to codeine and that something happened after you left?"

Sandra shook her head. "I don't think so."

"But it's possible," Crispin suggested gently, in a way that was more a question than a statement of fact.

"I ... I suppose," Sandra began, but then she stopped. "But, no. She wouldn't have taken them otherwise. And the charts didn't indicate any sort of allergies."

"What charts?" Spike asked.

"The records," Sandra blurted out. "I have medical records for all of you. They tell me about your allergies, your medical histories. Everything. I checked, but there was nothing in Janice's records to indicate she was allergic to codeine."

Bewildered faces looked around the room at one another.

"What are these records?" Spike demanded. "Where did you get them?"

Sandra looked at the faces staring at her. "They were here," she said. "When we arrived. Edwards has similar files indicating your food and drink preferences. I thought you had all filled them out. They were very thorough. Very explicit. Mr. Keill had them compiled when he knew who his guests would be and he left copies in my room to make sure everyone's medical histories were accessible in case of ... in case of ..."

She stopped and looked up with a frightened expression.

"In case of a medical emergency," Spike finished for her. "Is that what you're trying to say?"

"Yes." Sandra nodded. "I guess it is."

Spike looked around at the others. "I never filled out a medical sheet. Did any of you?"

Blank faces greeted him all around. The others shook their heads.

"I'd like to see these files," Spike said.

"Of ... of course," Sandra replied. "They're upstairs in my room."

Chessboard! the Voice suddenly hissed in Pete's ear. With a glance at the others, he got up from the table and went to the drawing room. There, on the board, sat nine chess pieces. A black queen had been set off on its side along with the knight and the pawn.

Pete turned and walked calmly back into the dining room where Sandra sat sobbing. Sami Lee and Max stood off to one corner watching her. The others had gone. Pete looked at them.

"Is she all right?" he asked.

Sami Lee shrugged. "Who knows?" She looked at Max. "I'm tired of this bullshit. I want to leave."

"I'm with you there, darling," he said. "We'll get Edwards to take us over this morning." He looked out the window at the ocean, where the waves were nearly four feet high. "If he can."

CHAPTER 13

Upstairs in Janice's room, David sat on the bed feeling for a pulse, but her arm was stone cold. Like the rest of her. He laid the arm aside and turned to Edwards.

"Must have happened a while ago. Sometime in the middle of the night, I'd guess, though I'm no doctor."

Edwards shook his head. "I can't believe this is happening," he confessed in a worried tone, dropping his professional demeanour.

"That's what I think," David said. "And I'm worried. You?"

Edwards nodded.

"So why were you in that video last night?" David asked.

For a moment, he thought Edwards wasn't going to reply. Then the man turned his gaze full on David.

"Because I was there," he said.

"At the party?"

Edwards shook his head. "Not exactly. I drove a cab back then. Around midnight, I got a call to pick someone up. Not at a house, but down the street around a corner. I didn't piece it together till later."

"Go on," David said quietly.

Edwards took a deep breath before he continued. "When I arrived, there were two guys waiting for me. They had a girl with them. She couldn't stand up. They said she'd had too much to drink. They waved a hundred in my face and said they'd give me her address if I'd take her home. Then once they got her in my cab they both took off."

"And they left a note saying to take her to a hospital," David continued.

"Yeah." Edwards looked at him. "How did you know?"

David made a face, but didn't answer.

Edwards continued. "I noticed the girl was breathing funny. I drove her to the nearest hospital, but I didn't stick around. I didn't want to get involved. I dropped her off outside emergency and left."

"Where she wasn't discovered for nearly half an hour ..." David said, looking down at Janice's dead body.

Edwards smacked the bedside table with his fist, making the lamp and a glass of water jump.

"Yes." He looked at David pleadingly. "I left her there with the note. How was I supposed to know it would get misplaced?"

David put a hand on his shoulder. "It's all right."

"It's not all right," Edwards said, shuddering. "It hasn't been all right for a single day since then. If I hadn't been such a coward ..."

David waited a moment then said, "I think ... we're in trouble here. All of us."

"You weren't in that video," Edwards said, watching David's face. "Or were you?"

"Never mind that. The thing is, we're all here now and we've got to figure out what's going on. I know it sounds ludicrous, but I think we've been set up."

"You mean ...?"

"I mean someone's brought us here to punish us. To kill us."

Edwards shook his head. "That can't be," he said. "It's crazy. It's insane."

"Exactly. My cellphone went missing last night and today everyone else is finding their phones have disappeared, too."

Edwards felt a shiver run through him. *I'd better tell him*, he thought, *before he suspects me of arranging this*.

"I took them …" he began.

"You what?" David said.

But before Edwards could finish his explanation, Spike burst through the door carrying an armload of file folders. Max and Pete were right behind him.

"Someone," Spike began, "has compiled medical histories for everyone in the house."

All eyes were on him.

"Look at these," Spike said. "Every major and minor illness I've had since I was born. And Max's lists his shellfish allergy." He looked at Janice's body. "Hers is here, too, but Sandra was right. There's nothing about a problem with codeine."

Verna was looking over his shoulder. "There's my allergy to wasps," she said, incredulously. "They even know about that."

At that moment, Edwards felt his phone buzz. No one noticed as he slipped out into the hall in all the commotion. He pressed "Receive" and his BlackBerry quickly downloaded the message.

It took only a second to read the two words. A dark look spread over his features. Now he knew for sure he'd been set up. He headed down the stairs.

He'd just reached the front door when Verna arrived.

"Everything all right?" she asked.

Edwards turned to her with a blank expression. "Yes — fine. I've got to go pick up Mr. Keill immediately," he said, remembering to smile reassuringly.

He went to the hall closet and pulled out a raincoat.

"Wait," Verna called to him. "Shouldn't someone go with you?"

"I will," said a voice behind her. It was Sandra.

"No." Edwards looked panicked. "No one's coming with me. It's too risky. The water's too rough. I'll be back in an hour with Mr. Keill and we don't want the boat overloaded."

With that, he rushed out the door and headed for the cove.

Spike had just come downstairs followed by David and Pete when they heard the boat engine start up in the distance.

"Where's Edwards?" Spike demanded.

"Gone to get Harvey Keill," Verna said.

Spike rushed to the door and looked out. The boat could be seen racing off in the distance. It was nearly swamped by waves as it pushed forward in the water and finally rounded the tip of the island, heading back to the mainland.

The others had come downstairs by this time. Their faces were uniformly stricken with worry and fear.

"What's going on?" Max demanded.

"We think it's Edwards," David told him.

"What's Edwards?"

Spike looked at Max. "We think he's been arranging these … these deaths."

"Murders," David's voice boomed around the room.

"It's probably revenge," Spike said. "Revenge for that girl's death."

"What are you saying?" Crispin called from the dining room where he sat with his hands on his tape recorder.

"That girl. The one who died of an overdose at Janice's party," David said.

"You know about that?" Sami Lee demanded.

"Edwards just told me. He was the taxi driver who took her to the hospital."

"What?" Verna said.

"He told me. Upstairs."

"Jesus," said Max.

David nodded. "He left her outside the emergency room door and just tossed the note beside her. It must have blown away before anyone found her."

"Oh!" Verna cried. "I can't believe this."

"And he was the one who took all our cellphones," David continued. "He just finished telling me he took them when Spike came in with the medical records."

"I hate this shit," Sami Lee said. She turned to Max. "Get us out of here, Maxie. Now! I want to leave."

"Fine," Max said, his anger barely controlled. "You find us a boat and I'll be in it in a second."

"Are you saying all our phones are gone?" Sandra asked.

"That's what Edwards said. 'I took them,' is what he told me."

"When did he do that?" Sami Lee demanded.

"I don't know," David said. "He just said he took them."

"So we can't even phone for help?" Verna asked.

A look came over David's face. "Wait a minute. He didn't get Noni's phone. He still had it on him when he died."

He raced up the stairs two at a time with Spike following right behind. The door was locked. Spike looked at David.

"Edwards has the keys," David said, in answer to Spike's look.

"Fuck that. It's just a door," Spike said.

"You really want to break it down?"

"Don't you?"

"Okay. Let's try it."

Taking turns kicking at the handle, they soon had the lock splintered. The door swung open on its frame. Noni's body lay exactly where they'd left him the night before.

David looked at Spike.

Spike shrugged. "Go ahead."

David went over and felt inside Noni's jacket pockets. He pulled out a wallet and a small notebook. The other pockets were empty.

"Shit! He got Noni's, too," David said.

"Are you sure?" Spike asked.

"Be my guest. Frisk the dead guy, if you don't believe me."

"I believe you. I just wondered if you were thorough. I'm not touching him."

"You carried him in here last night," David said incredulously.

"Yeah, well that was last night."

David bent over Noni's body and went through his clothing again. "It's not here."

The pair went back downstairs and looked at the grim faces assembled in the dining room.

"No phone," David said, shaking his head.

"We had to break down the door to his room," Spike added.

"We heard you," Max said.

"So we're cut off, then," Crispin said softly. "Unless" — he tilted his head toward the others in that peculiar manner he had of looking at a person while looking through them — "unless one of us has a cellphone hidden away that Edwards didn't dispose of."

"Anyone?" David asked, surveying the faces around him.

His question was returned with silence.

"Very interesting," Crispin pronounced in a solemn voice.

"Interesting?" Verna exclaimed. "It's not interesting. I think it's vile." She sat with a sulky look, arms wrapped around her pendulous breasts.

"Merely a clinical observation," Crispin replied.

"What about that laptop of yours, Crispin?" Spike said. "I saw you tapping on it last night when I went upstairs to bed. You left your door open a crack."

"I did?" Crispin asked with a start. "That's news to me. I had no idea my door was open. I shut it when I went upstairs after Mr. Embrem's death." He nodded softly. "Maybe Edwards came looking for my laptop, too. In any case, it's worthless for telecommunications. It has no wireless capabilities, I'm sorry to tell you. It serves as a word processor solely."

"So he murders two people and then gets away," David said.

"Of course, we may be jumping to conclusions," Verna said. "We don't actually know that anyone's done anything to anyone else to cause them harm."

"Don't we?" David said. "I think two deaths in less than twelve hours is more than enough reason to conclude that someone's been murdering the guests in this place. And the prime suspect has just fled the scene."

Spike turned to Sandra. "How well did you know Edwards?"

She shook her head. Her voice was faint. "Not at all. I met him on the boat yesterday when we all came over in the first group."

Spike nodded. "It's possible Edwards will turn up in half an hour with Harvey Keill and the new drummer in tow. But somehow I doubt it."

Pete had been sitting silently on the edge of the group. He started blubbering. "He won't be back," he said in a childish whimper.

"Why do you say that, Pete?" Max asked.

"Because," Pete said, "the chess game keeps changing."

"What are you talking about?" Max demanded.

Pete pointed in the direction of the drawing room. "Go check it. I was just in there. There are four pieces down."

The others looked at one another in bewilderment.

"What do you mean?" Verna asked.

"Let's go have a look," Spike said, with a glance at Pete.

They all wandered into the drawing room, Crispin following slowly behind. They stood staring down at the chessboard, which most of them hadn't noticed till now.

"When we got here, there were twelve pieces on it," Pete told them. "Eleven upright, and one down. Now there are four down."

They all looked at the board. Indeed, there were four pieces lying on their sides. A white rook had been placed alongside the black queen.

"There was one down when we got here. A white pawn. The second piece, a black knight, went down last night after Noni died," Pete continued. "This morning, when we heard about Sarah — or Janice — the black queen went down. And now the rook is with them."

Crispin shook his head. "I don't understand," he said. "What's this got to do with these deaths and whatever is going on around here?"

"Can't you see?" Pete shouted. "Every time someone dies, another piece gets knocked over."

He was nearly incoherent. He seemed to be frothing at the mouth as he spoke.

"How did you come to notice this?" Spike asked.

"I ... I count things," Pete said slowly, looking down at the floor.

"OCD," Sandra said quietly. "I noticed him doing some odd things yesterday with his hands."

"OCD?" said Verna.

"Obsessive-Compulsive Disorder."

Spike sighed impatiently. "That's just Pete. He's always been a bit off that way." He glanced at Sandra. "He did a few too many drugs back when the band was together."

"It's quite common, in fact," Sandra replied. "Many people suffer various forms of OCD. They need to count or touch certain objects or wash their hands frequently. It's usually an attempt to bring order to the world or to have some sort of control over one's environment in order to relieve anxiety."

"It sounds like crazy behaviour to me," Verna said with a worried look.

Sandra glanced up at her. "No crazier than cosmetic surgery."

"Oh!" Verna cried, her eyes flashing. "There's no need to be mean."

"I was just trying to explain various compulsions. You have one for perfection, it seems."

Verna was about to say something when she turned away.

"That's immaterial now," said Crispin loudly. It was the first time he'd raised his voice. "What we need to focus on is the fact that we are all stuck on an island in the middle of a fierce storm. If Harvey Keill and Edwards do not return later today, who knows how long it will be before anyone will come and rescue us? Did anyone see another boat in that boathouse? If not, then we will need to think about things like food, for instance. Do we have enough to keep us going for a while?"

Sandra looked over at him. "There was no other boat, but there seems to be a good supply of staples. Enough to keep us going for a week, maybe a little longer if we're conservative. I'm not much of a cook, however. That was Edwards's job, though I'll do what I can to manage for now."

"Good," said Crispin. "We'll all pitch in. I'm not very good at chopping and handling sharp objects, but I can manage to wash a pot or two when pressed."

"I don't wash dishes," Sami Lee snapped.

"Then perhaps you can dry them," Crispin said airily.

The others were looking at him, as if waiting for him to take over and tell them what to do.

"I hate to say it," the critic continued, "but I think we can safely assume Harvey and Edwards are not coming back, which means we need to make some basic plans. Who cooks, who washes, who keeps a look out to see if any boats pass by so we can try to flag them down. That sort of thing. We need to be practical. I'm sure we're capable of managing for ourselves until help arrives. It can't be that long before we're missed and someone comes looking for us."

The seven others in the room looked at one another and nodded in agreement, as though they too believed that their rescue would not be far off.

CHAPTER 14

The rain continued without let-up all morning. The next few hours passed slowly, but with each ticking of the clock it became increasingly clear that Edwards was not returning, with or without Harvey Keill, any time soon.

The remaining guests had gathered in the dining room. At noon, Sandra served a passable spread of cold cuts and bread with sliced tomatoes and a jar of mayo. She was right in saying she wasn't much of a cook, but the meal was filling.

At first there was little talk of the deaths. The subject was like the elephant hidden in the room until Verna brought it up, offering a small note of hope.

"If Edwards did murder those people," she said, "then we're safe now at least, because he's off the island."

"Until he comes back to finish off the rest of us," Sami Lee said, frowning. "He's probably crazy enough to do it."

For once, Sandra had eaten at the table with the others. She stood and went to put on water for tea and coffee. After she left the room, Crispin took the opportunity to address the others.

"I wonder if we really are safe," he said in a quiet voice. "We're assuming that Edwards is behind all this. Aren't we forgetting that Janice might have died from the medication Sandra gave her last night before she went to sleep?"

Max's eyes darted to the kitchen door. "You think it was on purpose?" he asked, his voice low.

"It could be," Crispin replied.

Murmurs of concern went around the table.

"I was wondering about Noni's so-called heart attack," David said. "What if it wasn't a heart attack? What if his drink was poisoned?"

Verna looked up. "He didn't have the wine, did he? Almost everybody else had wine or beer, but he had a special drink. Edwards made it."

"Yes," David agreed. "Edwards made it, but Sandra was in the kitchen at the time. She could have slipped something into his glass."

Glances went around the table again.

"Do you think they're in this together?" Max asked.

David shrugged. "It's hard to say."

The kitchen door opened and Sandra returned at that moment. The conversation died as everyone looked away.

"The kettle's on," she said, giving them a curious look. "Give it a few minutes."

Spike smiled. "You're a trouper," he said. "Thanks for looking after us."

David looked at the others. "We still have to consider the possibility that Edwards might try to return to the island when we're not watching." He stole a glance in Sandra's direction, watching her face. "I think we should do a thorough search later this afternoon, if anyone else will volunteer to come out and get wet with me. It might also be a good idea to set up a watch if we're still here tonight."

"Good idea," Spike said, glancing around the table. "Are we all agreed?"

"I'm game," said Verna.

"Sami Lee and me are sticking together, no matter what we do," Max spoke up.

"Agreed," David concurred. "I think we should all stick together from now on. Or at least go in small groups, to make sure we're safe in case he tries to sneak up and ambush us."

"You're forgetting one thing," Sandra said. "It would be very difficult for anyone to land on the island except by entering the cove directly in front of the house. He could never do it without being seen."

"Perhaps," David said. "But Edwards looked pretty fit. It wouldn't be too difficult for someone in his shape to shimmy up the cliffs on the far side — if he wanted to, that is."

"Yes, exactly — if he wanted to," Crispin broke in, his blue eyes looking at no one and everyone at the same time. "So let's keep in mind that if he wanted to do something like that, he would very likely have something extremely dire in mind. In which case, he might come armed."

This elicited a murmur of concern from the others.

"There's no doubt he'll know that we're on to him," Crispin added. "If he does return, he won't want to confront us empty-handed."

The faces that looked at one another around the table suddenly seemed to wake up to the potential threat confronting them.

"We're still assuming Edwards has something to do with these deaths," Max reminded them. "There's no direct proof."

"He stole our cellphones —" Spike began, but Max cut him off.

"Yeah, but he was also hired by Harvey Keill to bring us here. Where's Harvey? No one knows. First he says he's coming over in the afternoon, then next that he'll be here in the evening, and now it's this morning. But there's still no Harvey. So maybe Harvey told Edwards to take the phones once we got to the island. I'd say it's really Harvey behind all of this."

"But why?" Spike asked.

"Think about it. If we've hated him all these years for mismanaging the group, maybe he's hated us all these years for dumping him. Worse, we tried to turn him in when we found out he defrauded us of our earnings. But by then he had us all fighting one another. We never really talked about it privately."

"But we dropped the charges," Spike exclaimed. "Harvey kept all that money. We were the losers, not him."

Max shook his head. "Not entirely true. We lost our earnings, but Harvey lost his reputation. He hasn't worked with a hit group in more than a decade. All of his other bands dropped him like a hot turd when they found out what he'd done to us. As soon as they could get out of their contracts, they left him. He may have made loads of money on us, but his career was toast once it was all over."

"True," Spike agreed.

"Last night …" Max paused. "I don't wanna spook everybody, but last night while you were all in here eating, Spike and me were outside on the porch having a joint. After Spike left, I was sure I heard someone wandering around in the bushes behind the house. It was getting dark and I couldn't see too good, but I'd swear whatever was out there was human."

"You think Harvey's here on the island?" Spike asked, with a worried look.

Max's eyes shifted to Spike. "Harvey … or maybe someone Harvey hired."

"A hired killer," David murmured.

Verna shivered. "Is Harvey that powerful?"

"The question is," Crispin broke in, "is Harvey that crazy?"

Max turned his gaze on the critic. "Harvey is a law unto himself. I could tell you some tales that would curl the hairs on the back of your neck, but I won't go into it now."

There was silence as the wind blew against the house and rain pelted the windows.

"Still," Sami Lee said impatiently, "if we all stay together, we're safe from anything he might try. I mean, the bastard can't just come in here with a gun and shoot us all in cold blood."

"Why not?" Max turned to her. "I wouldn't trust Harvey as far as I could throw him, and that ain't too far. Remember, he's a big fat fucker. His main course in any meal was doughnuts."

Spike guffawed, but David cut him short.

"What's that smell?" he said, sniffing the air.

The others looked around.

"I smell gas," Pete said slowly.

A panicked looked spread across Sandra's face. "The kettle," she said, racing for the kitchen.

From the doorway, she could see the kettle sitting on the burner. There was no flame beneath. The air was rank with natural gas. She marched up to the stove and turned off the valve.

David came in behind her.

"Quick — open a window," Sandra commanded, grabbing a tea towel and waving it about.

David leapt to the nearest window and tugged. It was locked. He turned back to the dining room. "Nobody light a match!" he yelled. "We've got to get the air cleared in here. You should all go outside."

Everyone scrambled for the front door as David ran to the back door, propping it open. He helped Sandra waft the gas outside until the smell faded.

He returned to give the all clear to the others on the front porch.

"What were you saying about Harvey already being on the island?" David said to Max.

"You think Harvey did this?" Max asked.

"Well, somebody did," David replied. "Whoever it was must have come in the back door to the kitchen while we were all out here talking."

"Are you serious?" Verna said, a fearful look crossing her face. "You mean someone tried to blow us all up? That's horrible!"

Sandra joined them just then. "Actually, I'm not sure it was deliberate."

"What do you mean?" David demanded. "Someone blew out the flame and turned the burner on high."

They all looked at Sandra, waiting for an explanation.

"I set the kettle on the burner at full," she said. "I suspect it boiled over and put out the flame. There was hot water splashed over the stovetop. I think I may have overfilled the kettle a little. I'm not used to gas stoves."

"So you don't think someone snuck in the kitchen door while we were all out here?" Max demanded.

Sandra shook her head. "It's possible, but I don't really think so."

The faces around them looked relieved.

David shrugged. "Maybe not this time," he said. "But we still have to be vigilant. If nothing else, we now know how vulnerable we are here."

Sandra put a hand to her forehead. "I think I need to lie down."

They all came back inside to the parlour. Sandra lay on a chaise longue, her face pale.

Crispin spoke up. "I think it's time we had a frank discussion about everyone's involvement here. We've talked about how everyone got to the island, but we haven't really discussed why most of us were in the video accusing us of participating in that girl's death."

A silence fell over the room.

Crispin continued. "Or why some of us here are in it and not others."

Looks were exchanged around the room, but still no one spoke.

"Would anybody like to start?" Crispin asked.

The suggestion was again met with silence.

"All right. Then I'll start. I think I'm named in the video because I discovered the Ladykillers — at least in print. So far as I know, I fanned the flames that put the band in the spotlight ..."

"Hear! Hear! Good old Crispin!" Max cried, raising a fist in the air, but he settled back in his seat when his hijinks weren't returned with looks of amusement on anyone else's face.

"As I said," Crispin told them, "it was my article that helped the band on their sometimes-notorious rise to stardom."

"It's true," Spike interjected. "It's like you discovered us. If it hadn't been for you, we would never have been taken seriously by anybody, including Harvey. In fact, Harvey once told me it was your article in *Spin* that encouraged him to come out to the club that day. Otherwise, we'd probably still be just another garage band."

Crispin inclined his head. "That might be putting too fine a point on it, but I think I may have hastened the inevitable."

"So, in a way, you're responsible for the band's success," Max said. "But you weren't at that party when the girl died."

"No, I wasn't." Crispin concluded. "But I can understand why somebody might hold me responsible for what happened that evening."

"You're saying you agree with whoever is behind this?" Spike asked in a surly tone.

"What I'm saying is I can understand why someone might think that," Crispin replied calmly.

"But why would Harvey suddenly start to care about this girl who died?" Pete blurted out. "I mean, it was Harvey who got us out of that mess in the first place."

"Only because we were his meal ticket," Max said. "But not anymore."

Before anyone could respond, Sami Lee chimed in. "Does anyone even remember who she was? I mean, I remember all the trouble she caused, but does anyone else really remember her?"

Verna threw a shocked glance at Sami Lee for her callousness, but said nothing.

"That's right. She was just some chick who showed up at the party," Max exclaimed. "I don't even know who invited her."

"Spike did," Pete said.

Spike glared at Pete over his shoulder. "I might have. I invited a lot of people to a lot of parties back then. Most of them were glad for the invitations." He turned back to the others. "But Crispin wasn't at the party. Nor was Edwards, by the sounds of it, though we know from David what his involvement was in the events of that evening."

"I wasn't there," Sandra said softly, not looking at anyone.

"So that's three." Spike looked around the table. His gaze fell on Verna. "And you couldn't have been there or I'd remember you. I've never laid eyes on you till yesterday."

"Sarah was there. It was her party," Pete reminded them.

Spike nodded. "That's right. It was Sarah — a.k.a. Janice Sandford — who threw the party. She'd been a regular Ladykillers groupie for about a year by then. I think we all fucked her at one time or another." He looked around him. "No offence."

Sandra looked up sharply. "She said she felt guilty because she was in bed with you when the girl overdosed."

Spike shrugged. "I don't recall."

"Why did Janice throw the party?" Crispin asked.

"When she heard we were having a CD launch, she offered to host a little after-party at her place. She had this walk-up flat near the market in Seattle."

Max looked up sharply. "Sami Lee and me met at that party. I don't recall seeing this girl till she got sick."

Sami Lee nodded in agreement. "She was a nobody. I don't even remember her."

"She came backstage at one of our concerts," Pete said. "We all met her."

"Well, I never met her," Sami Lee said impatiently, lighting up a cigarette. "In any case, we know who gave her the ecstasy. That was Newt Merton."

Sandra looked up at the sound of the name. Merton? How had that fact escaped her all these years? She must have been stoned not to realize the man she sold prescription medication to was the same pusher who gave the dead girl her lethal drugs at the party.

Max nodded. "Newt was this kid who supplied us with stuff in the early days. He was the best, so we let him hang around the band. His dope was always pure, always quality, but I guess that night he got hold of some bad shit."

Spike shook his head. "They said it was the drug mafia trying to put the little guys out of business. Someone messed with his stuff that night and it was lethal. At least, that's what they made out at his trial."

At that moment, Sandra drew a line connecting the last few dots in the mysterious outline of events. She nearly gasped as she turned to David.

"Your last name is Merton. It says so on the file upstairs." Her voice was barely audible.

For a moment, David didn't speak. He looked at the faces staring at him.

"I knew it," Verna whispered.

"Whoa! I'm just a real-estate agent," David said. "I've never met any of you people before."

"It can't be him," said Spike. "He doesn't look anything like Newt."

"That's right," David said. "I don't know any of you, either."

"I know how we'll know for sure," Max said. "Roll up your sleeves."

David snorted. "You think I'm a junkie and that will prove I sold dope?"

Max leaned forward, speaking with a snarl. "No — I don't. But I remember Newt Merton had a tattoo of a seahorse on his left biceps. So let's see if you have the same tattoo."

David licked his lips nervously. He looked around the table.

"It can't be him," Spike said, watching David. "No way!"

"Show us," Max said. "Or we'll make you."

David sighed and rolled up his sleeve, revealing the outline of a seahorse on his biceps.

"Holy shit!" Spike exclaimed. "You're Newt Merton?"

"It's been a long time, Spike," he said. "People change."

"You're the guy who went to jail," Max said slowly.

"That's right. Four years of my life it cost me," David said darkly.

"It cost Zerin Ames more than that," said Verna.

David's fist smashed down on the coffee table, startling them all.

"Don't get all fucking high and mighty on me," he said through clenched teeth. "You guys invited me to that party in the first place. Anyway, I'm clean now. I haven't sold drugs for twenty years."

"Not since they put you in jail," said Pete.

"That's right. I went to jail for you fuckers, and don't you forget it. I pleaded no contest so the rest of you could get off."

"You got paid for it," Spike said. He looked around at the others. "In case anybody wonders why Newt went to jail without a fuss, Harvey concocted a scheme with Noni Embrem. They arranged to pay him fifty thousand bucks to go quietly. That's what was in the envelope Noni handed him before the trial."

David shook his head. "They only paid me to plead no contest. Noni promised me I'd get off with parole. He never said anything about going to jail."

"Tough luck," Max told him. "You gotta play the cards you're dealt."

David glared at him. "In that case, I had a crooked dealer."

Spike whistled. "So you must still be pretty pissed off about that. What's to say you weren't the one to do in Noni Embrem?"

David lunged across the coffee table as Spike retreated. Max and Pete restrained the real-estate agent, but barely.

"Get your fucking hands off me!" David screamed.

"Listen to me!" Max shouted. "If it's revenge you're after, you already got the guy who hung you out to dry."

"I didn't kill him," David said. "I didn't kill anybody!"

"Tell that to Zerin Ames," Spike said.

David spat at him. "Fuck you! That was an accident and you're all as responsible as me."

Spike shrugged. "The court decided differently. As for who killed Noni Embrem, you're the one who said Edwards took the cellphones. For all we know, you could have taken them to frame him."

"Go to hell!"

Max and Pete released David's arms. He slumped back into a chair.

"It's true," Verna said. "Edwards left after he got a text message telling him to come and pick Harvey up immediately. I heard his BlackBerry buzzing. I watched him read something. Then he left. As far as we know, he was intending to come right back."

"Then what happened to him?" David sneered. "Are you saying I killed Edwards, too? I'm still here. I didn't leave in the boat."

Verna looked at him sullenly. "I'm just saying it's easy to point fingers at people who aren't here, that's all."

"Well, you seem to have no problem pointing them at people who *are* here, sugar," David said.

Verna wrapped her arms around her chest and sat back, pouting.

"In any case, we're just discussing the possibilities," Spike said. "No one said you killed anybody."

"Well, discuss someone else for a change," David replied.

"If I may make a suggestion?" Crispin's elegant tones broke in.

"Go ahead, Crisp," Max said. He glanced around at the others. "We're all ears here."

"Thank you." Crispin nodded. "Clearly, it serves no purpose for us to start tearing one another apart. For all we know, this Edwards — if that's even his real name — could be heading back to get the rest of us right at this moment, with or without Harvey."

A few heads nodded in agreement.

Crispin continued. "I suggest we do a search of the premises for the cellphones, for a start, and then continue with David's original suggestion to search the rest of the island."

"A good idea," Max concurred. "Let's get started right now."

CHAPTER 15

They all agreed the obvious place to start was with Edwards's room. The door was unlocked and the room sparsely furnished. It held fewer designer touches than the guest rooms on the upper floors. The search took less than two minutes. Apart from a few articles of clothing, the dresser drawers were empty. A single suitcase stood upright in the only closet. It, too, was empty. No one had really expected to find a stash of cellphones hidden in the room, but they were pleased to discover the ring of master keys. It lay on the stand next to Edwards's bed, as though he'd left it there expecting to come back for it.

Spike was jubilant as he brandished it. "A fucking triumph, I call it. Yeah, baby! This way, when we lock our doors and go to sleep at night, at least we know he can't break in." He seemed thrilled at the prospect of beating Edwards at his own game.

"Now that we've got these, it should be easy to search the rest of the place," David said. He looked around at the others. "Are we all game?"

"Fucking right," Max said. "Why don't we start with the guest rooms?"

"Do you really think he might have been tricky enough to hide the phones in one of our bedrooms?" Spike asked.

"Who knows? I wouldn't put it past the guy," Max said.

They searched the entire house, starting with the third floor. Because of the building's minimalist design, it was quick work going through the dressers and drawers and looking under beds. There were no other possible hiding spots in any of the upstairs suites.

The only exception was in Verna's room on the second floor, where a heating duct lay partially unhinged in a corner nearest the window. They quickly unscrewed it using a quarter. Spike poked his head in the space. It hummed eerily. He looked around, declared it empty, and shut the vent again.

The search brought them back downstairs. They went carefully through the dining room, followed by the parlour. Verna, Crispin, Sami Lee, and Sandra sat and watched while Max, Pete, Spike, and David went over every piece of furniture and every corner of both rooms that might possibly provide a hiding spot. Still nothing.

The drawing room proved more difficult, partially because of the instruments set up on-stage. With some effort, Max, Pete, and David managed to lift the wooden platform a few inches while Spike looked beneath. It too was empty. They soon realized the cases housing the sound equipment would make a perfect hiding place for something as small as a cellphone, but again had to admit they were out of luck in finding anything. A further search of the mud room, hall closets, and various nooks on the ground floor failed to reveal anything of interest.

They looked at one another in bewilderment.

"I suppose he could have taken them with him," Spike said.

Verna shook her head. "I saw him leave. He didn't take anything with him. He just put on his rain gear and left. He seemed to be in a great hurry."

"There's nowhere else to look then," Max said. "They're not in the house. Maybe he put them in the boathouse."

Sandra stood. "I'll just go put the kettle on," she said. "I promise I won't fill it so full this time."

When she left, David snapped his fingers. "The kitchen! Of course — how could we be so stupid?"

Spike laughed. "Sure. That's where he spent all his time."

They barged into the kitchen, startling Sandra.

"Don't worry," Spike told her. "We're not here to bother you, but we've looked through the entire building and this is the last place where he could have hid anything from us."

Sandra turned the burner down low and left the room. The four men went through the lower cupboards and pantry in short order. David was the first to notice the lock on the cupboard door over the stove.

"There!" he said. "It's the last place left in the entire house."

Spike grabbed a nearby stool and stood on it. Most of the keys on the chain were for guest room doors, but there were three smaller keys. The second one opened the lock. Spike reached in and grabbed the canvas sack stuffed near the back of the cupboard.

"Gotcha!" he cried, shaking the bag as he lifted it down to David.

David reached in and pulled out several cellphones. He glanced up with a look of relief.

"I told you it was that bastard!" he cried.

Spike nodded. "Apologies, mate. I believe you now. Sorry I didn't before."

David shook his head. "It's understandable. But I didn't come here to kill anybody. I was duped by Harvey like the rest of you."

Max had his red phone in hand. He kept pressing the On button.

"Fucker's not working," he growled.

He grabbed a second phone and then a third. They all failed to respond.

"Fuck!" he shouted. "He's taken the batteries out of them."

David looked in the bottom of the bag then shook his head. "They're not here."

The faces looking at one another around the kitchen betrayed their fear.

David climbed back up on the stool and felt in the back of the cupboard. He pulled out a small metal container and shook it. There was something inside, but not batteries. He pried the lid off and sniffed the crystalline contents cautiously.

"I can't fucking believe it!" Max said, smashing his phone onto the tiled floor where it splintered and flew in pieces around the room.

"Of course you can," David said, stepping down off the stool. "He's planned this from the start. Who's to say Harvey even had anything to do with it?"

"Huh?" Max looked at him. "What do you mean?"

David held out the metal container. "I don't know for sure, but my guess is this is oxalic acid. Want to bet that's what Noni died of?"

Spike looked at him. "You still think this is all Edwards's doing? I'm beginning to agree with you." He turned to Max. "Did you even talk to Harvey before coming here?"

Max held his gaze for a moment then slowly shook his head. "No. I got a letter. You?"

Spike shook his head. "I got a letter, too. A fucking letter in the mail addressed to my real name, Elyot Jones. Who even sends letters anymore?"

Max let out a sigh of exasperation. "So you're saying Harvey might not even be behind any of this? You think it may all be this Edwards character?"

Spike looked at Pete. "Did you talk to Harvey, Pete?"

Pete just shook his head. The Voice was preparing to say something. He could feel the pressure mounting, but so far it hadn't spoken.

"So then it must be Edwards," Spike said. "But why?"

David spoke up. "I talked to him very briefly yesterday. I got the impression that he had an obsession with that girl's death. I think he blamed you for what happened after he dropped her off at the hospital."

"Why us?" Max asked.

David hesitated. "Because you two" — here he looked over at Max and Spike — "were the ones who delivered Zerin Ames to his cab down the street from the party. You were the ones who duped him into taking her to the hospital."

"But we left a note for the emergency ward," Spike said. "It was so they would know what she was suffering from. We couldn't know he wouldn't take her inside. Hell — we even paid the guy! We didn't know he'd panic and lose the note when he got there. That was his fault!"

"I doubt he'd see it that way," David said wryly. He thought for a moment. "Come to think of it, though, he didn't give any indication that he recognized me. So how would he know who I was? You guys didn't even recognize me at first."

"What does that matter?" Spike asked. "He's done his homework. You saw those charts listing all our medical histories, allergies, likes and dislikes. I think this is some sort of psycho mastermind we're dealing with here. Who knows what he's capable of?"

The wail of the teakettle interrupted their conversation. They heard Sandra's voice outside the door.

"I'll get the tea," she said. "Anybody for milk or sugar? Verna? Sami Lee?"

"I already told you, I don't eat sugar," Sami Lee said snarkily.

"Yes, I'm sorry. I forgot."

"Sweetener for me, please," said Crispin. "I'm diabetic."

"Yes, sorry," Sandra said. "I did remember that."

"Milk for me, please," said Verna. "If you can find any."

Inside the kitchen, the men heard Sandra approaching.

"Let's not say anything about the oxalic acid right now," David told them. He jerked his head in the direction of the next room. "Too upsetting."

"Agreed," said Spike.

Sandra entered the kitchen to find the four men staring at her.

"We found the cellphones," Spike said, nodding to the canvas bag on the countertop. "But nobody's going to be making any calls for the time being."

Sandra nodded with frightened eyes. "We heard you talking in the other room."

She busied herself with the tea tray and left the men to themselves.

Max tapped David on the shoulder and nodded in Sandra's direction. "It might not be a bad idea to keep an eye on her," he said quietly. "Till we figure out exactly what's going on here. You said yourself, she could be in on it with him."

David nodded and went over to Sandra. "I'll give you a hand."

She looked at him and shrugged. She hadn't forgotten his come-on last night. "I'm quite capable, but suit yourself. You can get the milk and sugar, if you want."

The others went back to the parlour. There was a sombre tone in the air. Outside, the rain lashed down on the trees and rocks with a tremendous weeping sound. Out on the ocean, the waves were tumultuous.

Spike stood at the window looking out. Maybe Edwards was all alone behind this, he reasoned. Or maybe Harvey and Edwards were together in trying to finish them all off and were just waiting out the storm before they returned. Or maybe this nonsense with the phones was really just another of Harvey's silly pranks and they'd all laugh about it in a day or two. Maybe.

A clanking from the kitchen distracted his thinking.

"Need any help in there?" Spike called out.

"Nah. We're fine," came David's reply. "Be out in a minute."

Sandra set out eight cups and saucers and placed them on the tray. David reached into the fridge for the milk while she poured boiling water into the teapot. The light in the refrigerator was off and it took a while to find the container in the dark. It lay behind several large juice cartons and a variety of beer bottles. As he reached in the back of the fridge, it occurred to him that it wasn't just the light that was off. The fridge was silent as well.

He set the jug on the counter for Sandra and looked in the space between the fridge and the wall. He could just make out the plug tilting at an odd angle in the socket. Maybe while they'd been checking the cupboard for the cellphones someone had jarred the fridge and the plug had come loose.

Sandra looked over at him with curiosity.

"Fridge is unplugged," he told her.

He groped around behind, feeling for the plug with his face pressed up against the cool of the fridge. He couldn't look at the plug and reach for it at the same time. In fact, there was just enough space for his arm to … there. He'd got hold of it. His fingers grasped the end as he reached around to plug it in.

It was at that precise moment that he recalled where he'd seen Verna before today. He almost laughed out loud at the realization, but then a sudden current of fear struck him like a stream of cold water. The more he thought about it, however, the surer he was. It would certainly shake them all up when he told them.

David felt the plug slip into place as a crackling sound filled the air. His scream tore through the house.

CHAPTER 16

The air was acrid with smoke when the others rushed into the kitchen. Everyone's first thought was that there had finally been an accident with the gas. David stared up from the expensively tiled floor, fumes issuing from his hair, his body still twitching. Sandra knelt and felt for a pulse. She turned to the others and shook her head.

"He's dead," she said simply.

"Oh, no!" Verna cried.

Just then, a strangled cackling caught everyone's ears. They all turned. Sami Lee stood in the doorway peering in. The sound came from her throat, as though she found the scene funny, but the crazed look in her eyes said her response was from shock rather than amusement.

Max put an arm over her shoulder. "It's all right," he said reassuringly, leading her out of the room. "It's all right, hon. We'll get off this island as soon as we can. We'll get far away from here."

Spike peered cautiously behind the fridge. Sparks fizzed and flew from the receptacle.

"David plugged it in," Sandra sobbed, a hand covering her mouth. "He said it was unplugged then he reached behind the fridge and plugged it back in."

Spike looked over at the kitchen counter. He picked up a pair of rubber dish gloves and put them on. Reaching carefully, he grasped the cord and pulled on it. The sparks died.

"I think we'd better leave it unplugged for now," he said.

"But how did it get unplugged?" Verna asked.

Spike looked over at Sandra, who stood alone near the stove. "Check that door for us, love."

She nodded and went over to the door. It was unlocked, though they had left it locked when they cleared the gas from the kitchen earlier.

"It's unlocked," she said, her voice trembling.

"But how ...?" Verna said.

"This was obviously set up by someone outside the house," Spike said in a grim voice.

"But how? Who did it?" Sandra asked.

"While we were searching the house for the cellphones, someone must have sneaked in and unplugged the fridge, making it look accidental."

They all looked out at the rain through the kitchen window.

"I think we'd better start that search of the island now, while we still can," Spike said.

Sandra looked over from where she had slumped against the counter. "I'll go with you."

"Are you up to it?" Spike said.

Sandra nodded.

Spike looked around at the faces watching him. "Anyone else?"

Verna nodded. "Yes," she said breathily. "I'll come, too."

Crispin said, "I'll go with you if you want me to." He'd been standing quietly without speaking all this time.

"Not you," Spike said. "No offence, mate, but you'll only hold us back. You stay safe inside with Max and Sami Lee."

"All right," Crispin said. "I'm sure I can trust them."

"Me, too," Pete said. He spooked them all a little. They hadn't heard him come back into the kitchen.

"We'll need something to protect us from the rain," Sandra said. "I saw rain hats and overcoats in the anteroom. I'll go find them."

She stopped and turned around to Verna. "Would — would you mind coming with me?"

Verna nodded. "Sure thing," she said. "You lead the way.

The two women went off together. Spike turned to look at Pete.

"I'll need you to help me carry David upstairs and put him in his room." He paused. "Are you okay to do that?"

"Yeah, I'm okay," Pete said, though he sounded anything but sure of himself.

Together, they hoisted the body and carried him up the stairs to the second floor, laying him on the bed in what had been his room.

Pete stood looking down at the blackened face for a moment. Spike stepped back and walked around to the other side of the bed.

Watch him! the Voice cried out.

For a moment, Pete thought David had come back to life and was addressing him. He looked down. The body lay there, eyes closed and unmoving.

Pete turned to see Spike watching him intently.

"Spooked?" Spike asked.

Pete nodded. "A little, yeah."

Spike came over and clapped him on the shoulder. Pete felt a tremor, as if he'd been touched by something evil.

Spike looked him in the eyes. "It's just a dead body, mate. No need to panic. Let's keep a clear mind and we'll all be fine till we get off this fucking island."

"Yeah — right."

They walked back downstairs together. As they were passing the drawing-room door, Pete heard the Voice again.

Count them! it said.

He felt a jolt of fear as he turned around. He already knew what he'd find.

"Look!" He stopped and pointed to chessboard. There were now five pieces down on their sides. A black bishop had been placed beside the rook.

"Who's been in here since this morning?" Spike asked.

"Everybody," Pete said. "We all have."

Spike shook his head. "Well, I don't know about you, but I can count only three dead bodies. Why do you think this has anything to do with anything?"

"I told you," Pete blathered. "Every time someone dies, another piece gets turned down. Who … who's doing this to us?" He sank to his knees, pulling at his hair. "Oh, fuck!" he screamed.

"Pete, get a hold of yourself," Spike said. "You're only making it worse for everyone else."

Pete looked up at Spike. "This is all your fault."

Spike grabbed Pete by the shoulders and shook him. "What do you mean by that?"

"You know exactly what I mean," Pete said menacingly.

"I don't know what you're talking about!" Spike slapped him across the face. Pete cringed and held his arms up in defence. "Now just shut up. We're not telling anybody else about this right now."

They continued on down the hall to the mud room, where Sandra and Verna had put on checkered jackets, and hiking boots. The rain gear was still hanging in a corner. The two men waited as the women brought it to the entrance.

Pete was paler than normal, Sandra thought. It was the shock. The four of them put the gear on over their clothes without a word then crossed to the front door.

They all glanced into the parlour through the open door as they passed. Crispin sat alone.

Spike stopped and looked at him for a moment. "We're going out now. We shouldn't be long. Will you be all right?"

"I'm sure I'll be fine," the critic replied, staring vacantly off into the distance.

"I'll tell Max we're going out and remind him that you're staying," Spike said.

He raced up the stairs and knocked on the green door. Max opened it immediately.

"We're having that look around the island now," Spike said. He glanced over Max's shoulder where Sami Lee sat silently rocking herself in a window seat. "Crispin's staying inside."

Max peered cautiously out into the hallway. "I'll come down with you and lock the door behind you when you leave," he said. "Sami Lee's scared. I want her to know she's safe in here. You'll have to knock when you want back in."

"All right," Spike said.

Sami Lee looked panicked when Max told her he was going downstairs. She clung to him and begged him not to leave. When he persisted, she agreed to go down with him. They closed the door behind the group and watched them trek off in the rain.

Max went to the parlour and looked at Crispin. "You're cool as a cucumber," he said "Doesn't any of this faze you?"

Crispin turned his head in Max's direction, but his eyes seemed to be watching something in a far corner of the room. He shrugged. "I can't control what's going on here, so I'm not going to waste time and energy getting upset over it. Someone will come for us eventually and we'll all get out of here. If we keep our heads, there's no reason the rest of us shouldn't be fine from here on. Now that we know what's going on."

"That's probably what Newt Merton thought," Max said. "At the very least, I think we should be wary of everything that goes on around us at all times. Don't trust anyone."

Crispin nodded. "A wise sentiment."

After a moment, Max said, "Can I get you a drink?"

A wry smile formed on Crispin's face. "You've just told me my life is in danger and I should be wary of everything and everyone around me, but you're offering to serve me a drink that I can't see you pour?" He laughed. "But yes, of course. Why not?"

Max went to the kitchen and returned with a bottle of wine and three glasses. He uncorked the bottle in front of them. The room was oddly silent except for the soft pull of the cork releasing and the hiss of the rain outside. Crispin fiddled with his recorder and stared off into the distance while Max poured. Sami Lee kept her eyes trained on the drowned landscape outside the window.

They sat and drank in silence. It was some time before anyone spoke.

"Any sign of them?" Max asked, finally.

"Nothing," Sami Lee said wearily.

Max began to sing softly: "On the first day of shagging, my true love gave to me a love song full of hate ..."

Sami Lee's frown stopped him dead.

"The Ladykillers' extremely memorable 'Love Song to Sid Vicious,'" Crispin said, stating the song's subtitle.

Max snorted. "What the hell were we thinking, anyway?"

"Why Sid?" Crispin asked after a moment.

Max shrugged. "We were all stoned on heroin at the time. It was just the thing to do back then. You know what they say — if you can remember the eighties, you weren't really there. I suppose thinking of old Sid came naturally. It's the way he chucked it, right? But what was in my mind while we were writing that song was how he killed his girlfriend, Nancy Spungen, in the Chelsea Hotel. I mean, it may sound crazy now that we've lived a little, but it all sounded so fucking glamorous at the time, if you can get into the headspace."

"I'm not sure I can," Crispin said archly. "Expressing violence in lyrics is one thing, but actually committing violence against another human being isn't that easy for me to understand. Maybe you could enlighten me as to how something like that could possibly be considered 'glamorous.'"

Max shot him a look to see if the critic was putting him on, but the expression on Crispin's face said he was deadly serious.

"How she died, I mean. You know — they were both strung out on heroin and lying in bed in the Chelsea and, I don't know — something must have happened between them, because the bugger stabbed her and then lay back down in bed and went to sleep. It's like total fucking End Of the World time and he doesn't even know he's done her in." Max looked around in exasperation. "Fuck — she was the one who got stabbed and even she didn't know it. So she, like, bled to death there in the bathroom while Sid was asleep in bed."

Crispin nodded. "And four months later Sid's mother killed him by shooting him up with a heroin overdose while he was asleep. Was that glamorous too?"

Max looked over. "Yeah? I never heard that bit."

"It was in a recent biography of the Sex Pistols. Sid's mother confessed just before she died of cancer. At the time he died, though, she said she found a suicide note from Sid saying he'd made a death pact with Spungen. I guess she changed her mind."

"Yeah? Holy shit!" Max exclaimed. "I always thought Sid's death was too convenient. The stuff that people do, huh? I heard one of Sid's biggest fans wrote him a note after the murder telling him God would forgive him if he confessed and sang Diana Ross songs."

Crispin turned his ethereal gaze toward Max, that unflinching, impenetrable stare. "We'll never know, will we?"

Outside, the rain continued to gust in a constant, cold stream. Four figures reached the centre of the island and stopped.

Spike turned to the others. "We'll do this boy-girl, boy-girl," he said. "It's safest that way."

He waited till they turned to listen to him, sheltered beneath their hoods and huddling against the cold and damp.

"What we need to do," he said, "is circle the island in opposite directions around the cliffs and then meet back here in the centre. It should take ten minutes at most. We'll be able to see everything there is to see that way. Remember that we'll never be so far apart we can't hear if the other team calls out. You might have to yell loud, but just do it. If we hear you, we'll come running."

The others listened, eyes wide, blinking away the rain.

"And don't try anything brave," Spike continued. "If you see Edwards or Harvey or anybody you don't know, just note where they are and come back and get us. Once we determine where they are and whether they're armed, then we'll decide what to do. Okay?"

Heads nodded.

"Sandra, you go with Pete. Verna, you come with me."

Spike watched as Pete and Sandra disappeared around a grove of trees. He turned to Verna.

"It's just you and me, kiddo," he said.

"Cozy," Verna said, heading in the opposite direction from Sandra and Pete.

As they moved along, Verna slipped on a rock and stopped to tie her bootlaces tighter. Spike went on ahead, pushing aside the branches of low-hanging trees. Verna noticed he was walking oddly. She couldn't remember having seen that before.

"You have a limp," she said, catching up to him.

He shrugged. "It acts up when it's cold and rainy, like now," he said. "I had a bout of polio as a kid. Not a severe case, as it turned out, but it left my right leg a little weak."

"Lucky it didn't leave much lasting damage," she said.

"Not to me, no. But my brother died of it. From what they can tell, I passed it on to him."

"That's so sad," Verna said. She hesitated. "My little brother died, too. Little Tyler."

They were making their way with difficulty through a patch of dense brush. Verna walked in front, while Spike followed behind.

"How did he die?"

"Motorcycle accident," Verna said. "At least it looked like an accident. I suspect otherwise."

"Tough luck," Spike said.

"He was troubled, my brother. I think he resented the kind of upbringing we had as kids, though we both went our separate ways by the time we were in our late teens. We didn't have a happy childhood and I think he couldn't face a lifetime of more of the same."

"Parents, huh?" Spike said.

"Yeah," was all Verna said in reply.

Spike's mother had given him no hint that she favoured his brother over him, but Spike felt the withdrawal of her affection after his brother's death. He hadn't been too young to make the connection. He grew up believing he'd killed his brother. His father had been an emotionally repressed blue-collar worker who never spent a great deal of time with his family. As a result, young Elyot managed to find ways to distract himself while he was growing up. Drugs, minor break-and-enters for which he never got fingered, and once a fruit-stand holdup that netted him a total of fifty-two dollars. The cops had come sniffing around his door, but ultimately he realized they had nothing to pin it on him, so he lay low till they went away. He never tried it again, knowing they were just waiting till next time. That was when he decided there wasn't going to be a next time.

At seventeen, he dropped out of school for good, but he'd already started a band and soon got a few gigs at local punk clubs. He met Max and Pete and Kent a few years later and joined their group, abandoning his own as too amateurish. The Ladykillers already had a repertoire, but they had just lost their singer, who got married and let his wife browbeat him into dropping out. Spike fit the bill. It was a match spawned in purgatory, as he liked to say when they finally broke into the industry full-time.

Spike's reminiscences were interrupted by something rustling in the brush off to the right. He held up his hand to shush Verna, but she was already aware of it. Her eyes turned on him, big and round with fear.

He pushed a branch aside and let out a yell as a large black shape leapt past him and tore off down the path with a growl. He was startled only for a moment before he burst out laughing.

"Fucking dog!" he yelled, his rain-streaked hair hanging down in strands. "I thought the fucker was going to kill me."

Verna watched him with a mildly amused look on her face, but said nothing. She cocked her ear to listen for sounds from Sandra and Pete, but all she heard was the rain coming down all around.

On the far side of the island, Sandra stood on the cliffs looking in the direction of the mainland. It couldn't be seen for the fog.

"You'd never know it was out there now, if you hadn't seen it with your own eyes," she said.

Pete stood off to one side. He hadn't said a word the entire walk. She looked over at him. He kept his head turned aside.

"I didn't mean to make fun of you about your OCD earlier."

She waited, but there was no reply.

"Do you want to talk about it?" she asked.

He shook his head. "Nothing to talk about," he said, and continued with their hike.

In the parlour, Max had just finished pouring the last of the wine into Crispin's glass. The critic held it up to his nose and sniffed. The recorder turned silently on the table beside him.

"I truly believe my sense of smell is that much stronger to compensate for my lack of sight," he said, with an air of satisfaction.

"Yeah?" Max said.

Crispin nodded. "If I told you I thought Sid Vicious was an unbelievably stupid twat, what would you say?"

"I'm not sure. Back then, I might have taken a swing at you, blind or not."

"Apart from killing his girlfriend, he once used soiled water from a toilet to shoot himself up with heroin."

Max guffawed. "Yeah — that sounds like Sid, all right. He did a lot of fucking stupid things. No more sense in him than … I don't know what."

"But you admired him?"

Max nodded. "Sure. We all did. It was like the Pistols gave us a licence to do whatever we wanted to do, you know?"

"Was that a good thing?" Crispin asked.

Max stared at him with incomprehension. "Of course! I never knew it was all right to sound terrible until I heard the Pistols, you know? They were just fucking awful and I ran home and played their record for Pete and my friends and I said, 'We can do that.' And we did."

"Your first recording was quite memorable," Crispin said. "It actually sounded like the Pistols."

"We were trying to sound like the Pistols, of course. Everybody did back then, but I liked groups like the Ruts and Stiff Little Fingers. Here on the west coast, we had the Germs. Stupid fucking Darby Crash with his passion for cutting himself with broken beer bottles. He couldn't do himself in fast enough once Sid was gone. It was like a fad for a while. Lots of people wanted to die." He nodded to himself before continuing. "I always thought the Clash was overrated, though. But you couldn't really imitate the Pistols. It was just impossible."

Crispin nodded. "How do you see music today?"

Max sneered. "Corporate bullshit. It's all marketing."

"Some would say that's all punk ever was in North America. A facade with a built-in marketing campaign and fashion to match. Rip a T-shirt and add a straight pin. And voila! You've got a punk movement. What happened to all that righteous indignation and anger?"

Max shrugged. "It went away, I suppose. You can't be angry forever. It was too destructive to last. But those of us who were there will always be changed by it. Punk wasn't just the music. It was a lifestyle. We lived it!"

Crispin sipped his wine. "How do you want to be remembered?" he asked. "What do you want people to say about you when you're gone?"

"I want them to understand that I'm not really nasty or vicious. I'm not a bad-ass. That was just the press making me out that way." He leaned over and kissed Sami Lee on the cheek. "I love my girl, Sami Lee. I always treat her right."

"It's true," Sami Lee said. She smiled grimly and took a drag of her cigarette.

"I like people around me to be happy — as long as they don't piss me off, of course."

Max smiled broadly before remembering Crispin was blind. He sighed and turned to look out the window.

The trek took Spike and Verna to the far side of the tiny island in less than ten minutes. They stopped to listen, but there was no sign of Sandra and Pete.

Verna looked worriedly at Spike.

"You don't think …?" she began.

"If they found Edwards and there was trouble, we would have heard something from them."

Verna looked meaningfully at him. "What if it's not Edwards?"

"Not a chance, "Spike said scornfully. "Pete's a bit odd, but he's not a killer."

"What if it's Sandra, then? She's a pretty hard-done-by lady. She definitely shows signs of addiction to something. I think she's pretty hardcore."

Spike lifted his head and howled into the rain. "Ha! Max is 'hardcore,' not Sandra."

"All right, but you know what I mean."

Spike stopped to consider this. "Yeah — I know. But I think somehow you're wrong. Tell you the truth, if anyone here is capable of murder, it's me."

Verna looked at him with a stricken expression. "That's a terrible thing to say at this moment."

Spike rolled his eyes. "Don't take me too seriously. Let's just keep on going."

As he stepped forward, the rock edge crumbled and he suddenly found himself sliding down the cliff. His hand grabbed a leathery cedar root. It was the only thing that saved him from falling over the edge.

Verna stared in horror.

"Don't just stand there. Help me!" he yelled.

Verna stood frozen to the spot, her eyes panicked. "Why did you say that?" she cried. "Why did you say you were a murderer?"

"Don't be fucking daft! I was only joking."

"How do I know?"

"Because I would have raped or killed you by now if I was the killer, you stupid bitch. Now help me up."

Verna grasped a branch behind her. Slowly, she reached a hand down to Spike. As he grabbed it, he yanked on her arm, pulling her toward the edge.

"I should kill you for that, you fucking twat!"

She stared in horror, trying to keep her grip on the slippery bark.

"But I don't want to die, so pull. Now!"

Verna pulled, keeping hold of the tree. For a moment, she wasn't sure if she could pull him up. Somehow she found the strength. With considerable effort, Spike was able to grab hold of a rock and haul himself up a few inches at a time.

He stood and brushed his hands off. A long cut bled down his arm. He turned to look at Verna.

"Next time, don't fucking hesitate!"

"You're fucking welcome," Verna said sulkily. "And next time you call me a bitch, I will let you fall."

She stomped off through the rain, heedless of the rocks and roots that stuck up everywhere waiting to trip an unsuspecting hiker.

Sandra and Pete had almost reached the halfway point when something occurred to Sandra. She stood on the edge and looked at the restless water more than twenty feet below.

"What if there are caves down there?" she asked with a mournful expression. "Edwards could be hiding out and we'd never see him."

"How would he get down there?" Pete asked.

She thought about it. "Ropes maybe. Or possibly his boat is tied up somewhere and we just can't see it."

She looked again and was startled to see something bobbing in the waves. Before she could make out what it was, she had a vision of Pete pushing her over the edge. She whirled to face him.

"Did you see anything?" he asked, staring at her.

She nodded. "I ... I think so."

They both looked together, trying to pierce the gloom and mist on the waves below. Something green bobbed under the water.

"There! Did you see that?" Sandra asked.

"What?"

"It looks like a knapsack or something."

Pete tried to lean over the edge to see what she was pointing at, but the rain obscured the view and cut visibility to almost nothing.

"It's green," she told him. "You can barely see it for the rain and the waves."

When Sandra looked again, it had disappeared, if it had ever been more than just a figment of her imagination.

They kept walking and met up with Verna and Spike a few minutes later.

"How'd you get that cut?" Sandra asked when she saw the gash on Spike's arm.

"This bitch tried to kill me by pushing me over the cliff."

Spike enjoyed the look of horror on Sandra's face. Verna shot him a nasty look.

He held up his hands. "Okay, I'm kidding. I slipped. Verna here was a true-blue hero. She hauled me back to safety."

"I can get you bandaged up once we get back to the house," Sandra said with relief. "There's not a lot in that first aid kit, but there are plenty of bandages."

"I'd appreciate that," Spike said. "Oh, by the way — we ran across a stray dog on our travels. He looks hungry. Scrawny son of a bitch and pretty vicious. We'd better tell the others to watch out for him."

"Are you sure it was a dog?" Sandra asked. "I hope it wasn't a wolf."

"Doubt it," Spike told her. "Too small for that."

"I wonder how he got here."

Spike shrugged. "Probably swam over at low tide or something. What about you two? Anything to report?"

Sandra shook her head. "Not really, but we were wondering … what if there are caves below the cliffs? Near the waterline? Someone could be hiding out there."

Spike thought for a moment. "I suppose it's possible. Is there any way to get a glimpse of them from above without having to shimmy down the side?"

"No," Sandra said. She looked over at Pete, who shook his head. "Pete and I both tried, but it's too dangerous. The only way we could do it is with a rope."

"There was rope in the mud room," Verna said. "Nylon, I think. So it would be fairly strong."

"I think I saw something down below," Sandra said. "I could just make it out floating in the water. It looked like a knapsack."

"Probably worth checking, then," Spike said, "but I can't do much of anything till I get this arm looked at. It hurts like a bitch." He threw a glance at Verna, but she didn't respond. "Besides, it'll be dark soon. We'll have to leave it until tomorrow."

They trekked back through the middle of the island, but found no trace of anyone. The trees were thickest on the cliffs. The centre was largely barren rock. Where the dog was holed up remained to be seen, but there were no other buildings and no possibility anyone could be hiding out in a hole or any other form of shelter. They checked the boathouse together, but it was empty. Life vests hung from the rafters — the ceiling was completely open and concealed nothing. Other than in the main building where the guests were staying, for all intents and purposes they were alone on a deserted island.

CHAPTER 17

Supper that evening was a sombre affair. Everyone agreed it was best to be wary of any possible avenue of attack. It was therefore decided that one person would cook while another watched. That way there could be no chance of slipping anything poisonous into the food.

Verna watched Max make an herbed chicken then she prepared a bean-and-vegetable salad. For all their outward desperation, the results would have been at home on the menu of any chic café.

Tea, coffee, and biscuits followed. By now Sandra had raised the simple act of boiling water to the level of an art. Conversation was stilted and intermittent. It was like a meal shared by religious postulants who have vowed to speak as little as possible. A few words surfaced now and again, and were responded to just as briefly, as the guests sank back into the tedium of eating in silence.

With dinner over, the seven turned their thoughts to the hours that lay ahead of them before sleep. It was a disquieting time, for the prospect of retiring to their rooms till morning — most of them alone — lay heavy on them all. Who might attack while they slept? Who might land on the island and lay siege to the house while no one was watching? Was it possible their tormentor might set fire to the place and leave them trapped inside to perish? They could all die and never be heard from again. It was terrible to contemplate.

It was Crispin who suggested they re-watch the video to determine a possible guilty party. They paraded by, those long-ago faces that now and then vaguely corresponded to people who were, or had been recently, among them on the island. Again, they listened to the video's theme song as the band thrashed out "The Twelve Days of Shagging" on that bygone Christmas Eve.

Count them, the Voice told Pete. And Pete did.

"Twelve," he said, when the video had finished playing and the images were laid to rest again.

"Of course there's twelve of them," Max spat out. "That's why it's called the fucking 'Twelve Days of Shagging.' Did you never stop to consider it before?"

"I don't mean the song. I mean the faces."

Max grunted. "Huh? What are you saying?"

Pete turned to look at him. "I'm saying there are twelve people named in the video."

"Play it again," Spike commanded.

Pete restarted the disc. One by one, they counted the faces: Harvey Keill, Spike Anthrax, Max Hardcore, Pete Doghouse, Sarah Wynberg, Jack Edwards, Sandra Goodman, Noni Embrem, Werner Temple, Sami Lee, Crispin LaFey, and Newt Merton.

"It's twelve in total, all right," Spike said, when the video ended the second time.

"I counted thirteen with Kent Stabber," Max stated.

Pete nodded. "Kent wasn't named, though. You saw his face, but his name wasn't onscreen."

"That's right," Spike said. "He was in the band, but he wasn't named in the video."

"Why is that?" Verna asked.

"Because he's already dead," Pete said agitatedly. "That's why there's only twelve. Twelve faces, twelve verses, and twelve chess pieces."

Spike turned to him. "And you're suggesting there's a connection?"

"You're not listening to me!" Pete exclaimed. "I already told you, every time someone dies, another piece of the chessboard gets turned over."

"I am listening to you. And just because you told us that, doesn't make it so. As I recall telling you earlier, there have been only three deaths —"

"That we know of!" Pete insisted.

"All right — three deaths that we know of," Spike amended. "So why are there five pieces lying down on the board?"

"I don't know," Pete replied, sinking back in his seat.

"And even if whoever is doing this eventually murders everyone on this bloody island — which he bleedin' well won't — that still only makes ten in total. So no Twelve Fucking Days of Murder, is how I read it. So bloody well stop this nonsense."

"Eleven," Pete said.

"What?"

"Eleven — if he kills the rest of us. You forgot Edwards."

"All right," Spike said testily. "So I forgot Edwards. Who's the twelfth?"

Pete shrugged. Sometimes he wished the Voice would provide him with useful information and not just commands to count this or do that. It might make things a lot simpler. It would be like having a personal news service to keep him briefed on current events.

"Who fucking cares how many have already died?" Sami Lee exclaimed. "We're the ones who are still alive. What are we going to do about the rest of us here?"

Spike held up his hand. "The most important thing for us now is to stick together."

"And how are we going to do that?" Max demanded. "You think we should all sleep in one bed? Not bloody likely."

They argued over various permutations on sleeping arrangements, but in the end decided it was preferable to stick to their own rooms. Despite everything, it still felt safest to sleep behind a locked door. It was with heavy looks of dread that they all went upstairs at the very early hour of nine o'clock that evening.

"And I don't need to remind everyone to lock their doors and not open them till morning," Spike said. "Unless — unless anything happens during the night. If something happens, just let out a howl and the rest of us will come running. Agreed?"

Reluctantly, they all nodded one at a time.

"Wait a minute," Verna said. "What about the key ring?"

"Bloody hell!" Spike exclaimed. "Of course. There's a spare key to every single bedroom."

"What'll we do with the keys?" Sandra asked. "We can't put them in the hands of one person — just in case, I mean."

"We could all take our own keys to bed with us," Verna said.

Spike threw her a scornful look. "And if anything happened, we might not be able to break into your room in time. It's not like we're as young as we were back in the days when we used to trash computers and appliances on stage."

"Oh!" Verna slumped back in her seat.

It was Crispin who solved the riddle. "If I may suggest something, I believe you said there were two keys to cupboards in the kitchen …"

"Three," said Spike. "There were three."

"No matter," Crispin said. "Here's what I propose: I have a case that locks with a key. If we put the ring of keys in there, I can give the key to one of you. Then we lock the cupboard, and we give that key to another one of you. Therefore it would require two keys to get to the ring, and no one person will have control of or access to it.

Although he couldn't see the faces staring at him, he sensed their approval of his rather ingenious solution to the problem.

"Then we need to give the keys to two people who don't know or particularly trust one another," Max said.

"I don't know any of you," Sandra suggested quietly.

"Okay," Spike agreed. "Who else?"

He looked around. Several people shrugged.

Verna said, "I'll do it. If you all agree."

There were no dissenting voices, so Spike placed the ring of keys in Crispin's satchel. He then locked it and handed the first key to Sandra.

"Sandra has the key to the satchel," he announced. "And she will keep it in a safe place without telling the rest of us. Now let's put the case in the cupboard downstairs."

When that was done, he handed the second key to Verna.

"Verna will now put the key to the cupboard somewhere safe where none of us can find it and she will tell no one," Spike announced again.

"And we will all go to bed and sleep safely and soundly and, we hope, not wake till morning," Crispin added.

"Shall we all agree on a time to get up and unlock our doors in the morning?" Sandra asked. "I only think it's sensible."

"You're right," Max said. "How about we all get a good night's sleep and stay in our rooms till eight o'clock?"

The suggestion was agreed upon by everyone. And with that they all trudged up the stairs, shutting and locking their doors behind them.

CHAPTER 18

In the morning, breakfast was prepared and eaten communally by seven miserable, grim people. The coffee helped lighten the mood a little, but the steady rain outside the window predicted yet another day, and possibly another night, of being stranded on the island.

From the faces surrounding him, Spike could tell that no one had had a great sleep. He hadn't slept at all. His arm felt better, but he'd helped himself to the crystal meth in the bowl in the parlour and stayed up all night, his mind a phantasmagoria of evil-looking creatures and paranoid thoughts.

"First things first," Spike said, running his fingers through his hair. "I think we need to do another run of the island to make sure Edwards hasn't returned. At the same time, we should investigate the knapsack or whatever it was that Sandra saw floating off the west end of the island yesterday." He looked at Max. "And I think this time, you should help, Max. We're going to need your muscle to help me get down the cliff."

Max turned a sullen gaze at him. "Who appointed you fucking king-shit leader of this shithole?"

"Do you have a better idea?" Spike snapped. "Or do you just want to sit here and wait till they come and get us?"

Max shrugged and turned to Sami Lee.

"Will you be okay while I'm gone?"

"I'll be okay," she said, lighting a cigarette.

Sami Lee, Verna, and Crispin stayed behind in the house. One by one, Spike, Max, Sandra, and Pete suited up and trekked outside. Spike grabbed a long coil of yellow nylon rope as they left. The rain wasn't as heavy as it had been on the previous day, but the mist hung thick in the boughs of the trees overhead.

"Watch out for that dog," Spike warned. "He's got nasty teeth."

Before long, the foursome was thoroughly soaked as they pushed their way through the scrub past the low-lying branches of cedars. It was slippery going on the rocks.

They split up in the same location as on the previous day, with Spike and Pete taking the alternate route this time, while Sandra and Max went the other way around. There was no sign of the stray dog, though more then once Sandra sensed it following them and keeping track of the humans who had invaded its home.

As agreed, they met again at the far end of the island near where Sandra had seen the floating object.

Spike looped the rope around a cedar trunk, making a primitive pulley. He looked at the others.

"Anyone want to volunteer to make the first flight?" he asked mockingly. "No?"

"We'll stay here and make sure the tree doesn't pull out of the ground, Spike," Max told him tauntingly. "Someone's gotta have your back."

Spike grunted, whether in agreement or resignation. He tied the rope around his waist and tossed the other end over the cliff, slowly lowering himself down.

They waited and watched as he slipped from view, taking care not to stand too close to the edge should the rock crumble and take them all down with it. Spike seemed to disappear in the mist as he got closer to the surface of the water.

After a minute, they heard him call up.

"I see something. Sandra's right — it looks like a knapsack."

There was silence for a minute. The rope strained as Spike descended farther.

Suddenly, they heard him shout, "Holy shit!"

The rope zig-zagged wildly for a moment as though he might be fighting with something at the other end.

"What is it?" Sandra yelled down. "Are you okay?"

For a moment, there was no answer. Then Spike replied. "Give me a minute. Fucking hell. I'll tell you when to pull me back up."

They waited as the rope turned and settled. Then Spike called up.

"I'm ready. Pull me up."

After a good deal of sweating and cursing, Spike's head appeared, followed by the rest of him, soaked to the skin. He collapsed in a heap. For a moment all he could do was lie there and shake his head. Finally, he pushed himself upright.

"What was it?" Sandra asked, agitated. "For god's sake, tell us!"

"It was Edwards," Spike said slowly and quietly.

"What?" a chorus of disbelieving voices cried out.

"He's drowned down there. I tied the other end of the rope to his body. We'll have to pull him up."

With more sweating and heaving, they pulled on the rope till Edwards's body appeared and flopped onto the rocks at their feet. They all stood looking in horror at his battered face.

"I saw an oar as well," Spike said. "It looks like he didn't make it very far. His boat must have been swamped."

Max glared. "And all this fucking time we've scared ourselves shitless thinking he was coming back for us. What fucking idiots we are!"

"No, Max," Spike said. "We made a logical deduction. It seemed likely it was Edwards, and we left it at that. So now it looks like it's been Harvey all along."

"Fucking Harvey!" Max screamed, kicking at a tree root.

Sandra turned to them. Her voice was quietly terrified. "Who's to say he wasn't coming back to get us in the middle of the night?"

The faces that stared at one another betrayed a combination of anger and bewilderment. Spike knelt beside the body and felt around inside his jacket pockets.

"What do you think you'll find?"

"Edwards left here yesterday with the one working cellphone on the island. Maybe he's still got it on him …"

He gave a triumphant yell and pulled out a plastic-encased BlackBerry. He pressed the On button and watched, barely able to stifle a cry of jubilation as the screen lit up. They all watched hopefully as the logo came up and disappeared, followed by the normal display. On it, they read two words: *You're next*. It was dated the morning of the previous day.

"Oh, shit!" Pete said.

"That's why he ran," Spike said. "He decided to get out while he could, and left the rest of us here to face it. At least he did us one favour — now we can phone for help."

Suddenly, the text faded. The screen sputtered and died.

"No way!" Max roared.

Spike shook the phone. He powered it off and pressed the On button again, but it refused to restart. "I don't fucking believe this," he said in a weary voice.

Sandra moaned and dropped to a crouch. She sobbed and wrapped her arms around her knees. No one made a move to comfort her.

Endgame, said the Voice in Pete's ears.

After a few minutes, Sandra shook her head and stood up. "We'd better go," she said.

Between them, they hoisted Edwards's body and carried him through the trees back to the house. Verna was waiting for them. She opened the door as they climbed the steps. No one spoke as they carried Edwards into his former room behind the kitchen.

"How many more bodies are we gonna stow away before this place starts to smell to high heaven?" Max asked.

Spike shot him a look. "We aren't going to be there that long, so don't worry about it. Besides, we can't just leave them out in the rain. The dog might get at them."

Verna shivered. "Four," she said ominously. "That's four of us now."

Pete nodded. He was thinking of the five downed chess pieces. "On the fourth day of shagging, my true love gave to me four oceans to drown in ..."

"No!" Verna's hand went up to cover her mouth.

Spike looked at Pete, speechless for once. After a moment, he said, "What are the others again? Five tongues of fire ..."

"David died of electrocution," Verna said in a tearful voice.

"Three evil Jujubes ..." Spike sang softly.

"And Janice died when she took the codeine pills," Verna supplied.

They stopped and looked at each other.

"Nobody's been shot, though," Spike said, sounding a little bit relieved. "No silver bullets."

Sandra gasped. "The recipe!"

"What recipe?" Pete asked.

"For the drink ... the drink Noni asked for. I saw it when Edwards was making it. It's called a Silver Bullet. What he drank was a Silver Bullet."

"Fuck me," Spike said.

"And a love song full of hate ..." Max filled in. "That's for all of us, is my guess." He turned to look at Verna. "Except you, sister. How come you're not named in this little charade?"

Verna stood there, eyes wide. "I don't know."

Max watched her for a while then said, "I don't believe you. You're connected with this sordid fucking history somehow, unless …" Here he stopped and looked around at everyone else in the room. "Unless you're the murderer, of course."

He let the statement hang in the air.

"I'm not …" Verna said breathlessly. "I'm not a murderer," she repeated, looking at all of them.

"Then who are you?" Spike said, following Max's lead.

"Her name is Verna Temple, according to my files," Sandra said.

Spike's head jerked up. "Temple?"

"Yes," Verna said. "My name is Temple."

Spike sat back in his chair and watched her with narrowed eyes. "Now isn't that a coincidence? That's the same last name as that kid who used to hang around with us." He snapped his fingers. "What was his name, Max?"

"Werner," Max said.

"That's it," Spike said. "Werner Temple. Have you got a brother, Verna?"

Verna shook her head. "He died." She looked at Spike. "I told you that yesterday."

Spike shrugged. "So you said."

"But it's true!" Verna cried.

Spike glared at her. "You also said his name was Tyler."

A panicked look spread across Verna's face. "That's true. His name was Tyler."

Without warning, Max slapped her cheek.

"Think again, Verna. Have you got a brother named Werner?"

She put a hand to her face and shook her head.

Max slapped her a second time while the others watched. "I'm gonna ask you again, Verna, and I want to hear the truth. Do you have a brother named Werner?"

Verna looked up fearfully, her lipstick smeared and hair dishevelled. She rubbed the back of a hand against her mouth to wipe away the blood.

"Please don't hit me agai—" she began, as Max's hand smashed against the other side of her face. She screamed.

"Whether he's dead or alive, I wanna hear you tell us that you have a brother named Werner."

"I don't have a brother named Werner," she began, but her words were stopped dead as Max slapped her harder.

Verna sobbed and shrieked, "My brother is dead. My brother is dead!"

"Werner is dead?" Max asked.

Verna hesitated then shook her head, *no*.

"So Werner is alive?" Max asked.

Again, she hesitated before shaking her head, *no*.

Max raised his fist to hit her again, but Spike stopped him.

"No," he said. "This isn't helping."

"The fucking bitch is playing games with us, man!" Max shouted. "I'm gonna fucking beat it out of her if I have to kill her."

He made to strike her again, but Spike stopped him. Verna screamed and fell on the floor cowering, her arms over her face.

"No, no," she sobbed. "My brother is …"

"Your brother is what?" Max demanded. "Tell us what Werner is."

"Don't make me say it …"

"Say it. I want to hear you say it."

"Werner is … Werner is … me."

There was a stunned silence in the room.

"I'm Werner," Verna sobbed quietly. "I'm Werner."

Max grabbed her arm and pulled her to her feet. "You're what?"

Verna shook her head and took a deep breath. "I'm Werner Temple. I'm Verna Temple."

"Fucking hell," Spike said.

Max looked her over. "Holy shit," he said, and let go of her wrist.

Verna stood upright on her own. She smoothed her clothes and looked around at all of them.

"I'm … I used to be … Werner. Now I'm Verna."

CHAPTER 19

Although none of the guests trapped on Shark Island would ever see it, a small notice appeared in that morning's edition of *Noise* magazine, along with the other more prominent music tabloids. Except for *Noise*, where it was featured in a news brief on page two, the announcements were buried at the back of the other magazines alongside the tail ends of longer articles. The news was not considered worthy or important enough to be given more prominence, but was simply meant as an epitaph to an era of excess and deceit that had coloured the music industry in a time now past.

The article read as follows:

> Harvey Keill, 54, band manager, was found dead in his Chicago apartment on September 20 just before noon. His cleaning lady, who discovered the body, said he hadn't been answering her calls for at least two days prior.
>
> Keill was once considered a superstar manager, but in recent years his star faded until he was little more than a half-forgotten legend. In his day, Keill was credited with having created the Ladykillers, a group that would form the basis of a punk-rock revival in the late eighties and early nineties. The Ladykillers broke

up amidst a storm of controversy, both personal and financial, in the late nineties.

An unsubstantiated coroner's report suggests Mr. Keill died ingesting a poisonous substance mailed to him inside a CD case. A CD containing a copy of the Ladykillers' hit, "The Twelve Days of Shagging," was found at his desk alongside a half-full box of Krispy Kreme donuts.

A full investigation is pending.

Had the news in fact reached Shark Island, the announcement still might not have been believed, as much as it might have helped round out Pete Doghouse's theory of twelve intended murder victims. To the seven people trapped on the tiny piece of rock in the middle of Puget Sound, however, the presence of Harvey Keill still seemed to be very much alive and well.

"Just another bad publicity stunt," Spike Anthrax would have said, had he heard the news.

And he might have convinced them that this too was true.

CHAPTER 20

Everyone helped with the evening meal, which was comprised of canned food that simply had to be heated and served. Crispin was exempt from the preparation, but asked to be given the task of setting the table.

"If you will be patient with me, I can at least do that," he told them. "Though the colours may not match entirely. However, I would like to feel as though I have contributed in some small way."

They left him in the dining room. Sami Lee, cigarette in one hand and dishes in the other, went back and forth bearing plates and silverware, leaving them on the sideboard for Crispin to sort out.

Supper was an even more sombre affair than the previous night's. Verna was last to arrive, her hair piled on top of her head and silver hoops dangling from her ears. While she hadn't been entirely successful in covering her bruises with makeup, the dress she wore revealed her cleavage in a way that put the lie to the fact that she'd ever been anything but a biological woman.

The room fell silent as she entered. Max looked up.

"I'm sorry I hit you," he said, before turning away again.

Verna nodded. "Apology accepted."

She paused a moment then addressed the gathering. "I'm sorry I lied to you all. Or rather, that I did not disclose my true identity. One of the things you learn during the transitional period is to let go of your old self and merge fully into the new you. It's impossible to live two lives at the same time, so most successful transsexuals simply abandon the past and any reference to it that might hinder their progress in becoming the person we know we are meant to be."

She looked around at the others then continued, "Some of you knew me as Werner, but Werner is no more. Just as I also had a brother who died when I was very young. Although I honour their memories, I know and accept that both are gone."

"Noble sentiments," Spike said when she finished. "If you were so determined to leave the past behind, then why are you even here? Aren't we Werner's past? You said you won a contest. Why did you enter?"

For a moment, it seemed Verna wasn't going to answer. A hand went up to tuck a strand of hair behind her ear. Then she spoke.

"There's always a moment when someone makes the decision — to change their sex — and mine had to do with this band." She looked around the table. "I met most of you when I was nineteen. I hung around with you for a couple of years. You were fun, exciting, and you seemed to accept me for who I was. Then I fell in love with Max …"

"Oh, fuck you," Max said.

"And you did — many times, in fact."

Max clenched his fist and looked around at the others. "It was the fucking heroin. I didn't know what I was doing." He looked over at Sami Lee. Her face was frozen in a sullen grimace.

"I apologize for bringing this up in front of everyone," Verna said. "But it's true."

Sami Lee looked at Verna. "It's not like it's news. Max's dick was never very exclusive."

"So I learned. Nevertheless, I fell in love with him," Verna repeated softly. "I didn't plan it. It just happened. I also helped you with some of your music, as I'm sure you recall."

"What of it?" Max snarled.

"You let me help you when you saw I had some good musical ideas. I didn't ask for anything in return. I just wanted you to love me. That's all."

"Just." Max sneered. "Don't listen to her. Him — it. This is bullshit." He turned suddenly to Crispin. "Turn that fucking thing off."

Crispin's hand crept over to his recorder.

"No — don't turn it off," Verna said. "This is as much my story as it is Max's. I want it on record."

The hand retreated from the recorder.

"And it's not bullshit," Verna said sharply. "I helped you write some of the songs that made you famous. Maybe not in a big way, but in little, telling ways. I came up with the chorus on the song that became your first big hit."

"'A Kiss Is Just an X'?" said Crispin, stunned. "That song is a classic!"

Verna kept her gaze on Max. "That's the one. Remember, Max? What I suggested gave it the hook everyone still talks about when they mention that song. I helped make it a hit."

"Is this true?" Spike said to Max.

Max's eyes narrowed. His jaw was tight.

"Yes, it's true," Verna said. "I didn't want anything in return for it. I was glad to help, but Max wasn't going to let you know I had anything to do with it. He said the song had to have his name on it, because of the band, but that he would give me credit for my contribution one day. He never did."

"Fine!" Max said suddenly. "You want credit? Here it is: you helped me with the fucking song. You want money, talk to Harvey. He stole it all."

"I don't want money," Verna said softly.

"Then why are you saying this now?" Max said.

"Because I think … I think it's time to say everything." Verna turned to the others. "All of us. If we have anything to say about what happened back then, it's time to say it. We're not going to get another chance."

"What's that supposed to mean?" Spike said.

"It means that none of us are going to leave this island alive," Verna said breathily.

A chorus of dissent went up around the table, but died just as quickly as it arose.

"You're wrong," Max said defiantly. "I am getting out of here alive." He looked over at Sami Lee. "And so's she." He looked around again. "What happens to the rest of you is up to you. If you're smart" — he looked at Verna — "you won't trust a thing she's saying."

Verna held his gaze. "I became Verna for you, Max. Like it or not, it's true. I knew you didn't love me as Werner, so I became Verna. So you could still hang on to your stupid badboy of rock 'n' roll façade and no one would be the wiser." She looked at Sami Lee. "But you chose her instead. I didn't understand it, but I accepted it."

"Well, whatever you did it for it was a waste of time," Max said. "Because I don't even like you now."

"I know that," Verna said. "I can see that. But at least now I'm proud of who and what I am. Back when I was Werner, I was just something for guys like you to screw and then go back to their girlfriends and deny it the next morning. At least I know who I am now."

"Congratulations," Max said. "I hope it makes you happy. Anything else you'd like to confess?"

They all waited as Verna looked around the table.

"Yes, there is. I'd like to confess that it was my idea not to call 911 that night when Zerin Ames was dying. I did it to save Max.

Not that it matters now. But I thought if anything got into the news or if the police got involved, he might go to jail."

There was a long silence.

Verna continued. "You all know what part you played in that evening. If you want to make peace with your consciences, then now's the time to do it. As I said, none of us are leaving this island. I can feel it."

"Maybe you got plans to make sure that happens," Max said. "You can't even decide what sex you are. How are the rest of us supposed to trust you?"

Verna shook her head sadly at him. "Can't you even admit that it was you who dragged her out to the cab that night and left her with an unknown person to drive to the hospital?"

"Fuck you!" Max said. "At least I took her out of the house and tried to put her in the cab. You didn't even do that much."

"I know," Verna said softly. "I'm not denying it."

Max stood and tossed his napkin on the table. "I'm not hungry anymore."

After a moment, Spike followed him out onto the front deck. They sat and smoked a joint.

"Now what are we going to do?" Spike asked.

Max grunted. "I'm getting the fuck off this island. Tomorrow — even if I have to swim."

"So much for a career revival," Spike said.

Max shrugged, but said nothing.

"We're fucking has-beens," Spike said. "Time to admit it, Maxie boy. We had three hits in ten years, including that piece of shit, 'A Kiss Is Just An X.' Forget that fucking Verna or Werner or whatever her name is. That wasn't punk — that was fucking disco, man. Dance-hall shit. Sentimental crap. It was a joke!"

"Yeah, except for that very catchy chorus," Max said with a snarl.

"Right. Lest we forget. It wasn't even ours." Spike stared off into the distance for a while. "It's all over, man. Vicious died at twenty-one. Cobain at twenty-seven. We should have done the same. The best was already behind us."

Max thought this over. "What about Dylan? He's twice our age and sounds like total shite, but people still buy his records."

Spike laughed contemptuously. "Bob Dylan is a fucking mega-superstar with a fifty-year recording career behind him. We're has-beens at fifty. Even Lennon was dead at forty."

Max grumbled. "Fucking Beatles. You were always going on about the Beatles. What did the fucking Beatles ever do?"

"Besides create the template for modern pop music?"

"Yeah — right. Remind me again. How did John Lennon die?"

Silence crept in around them. Max reached over and shook Spike's shoulder. "What happened to you, man? Why did you just give up?"

Spike shrugged. "I lost my nerve."

"You did not lose your nerve," Max said. "Never. Not you."

"You're right. First I lost my voice and then I lost my recording contract. And then I lost my nerve. It didn't take a genius to figure it out. I was through."

"But you just gave up. Why? You should never have let it all go."

Spike looked off in the distance. "One night ... I saw that girl ... Zerin Ames ... out in the crowd. It was one of our last concerts. I was singing and I looked out over the heads and there she was. My voice went dead. I couldn't go on. I don't know if I really saw her or not, but it sure as hell looked like her."

Max turned to him. "You're telling me the great Spike Anthrax saw a ghost and had a pang of conscience?"

"I got the spooks, man. I just couldn't go on after that."

Max shook his head. "We thrashed, man! We were the fucking best."

Spike nodded. "Yeah — we thrashed."

"We were the Sid Vicious and Johnny Rotten of North America. People like us don't give up. We're lifers in this business. We shit and piss music."

There was silence for a while. The roach moved back and forth between them.

"Do you really think it's Harvey doing all this?" Max said at last.

"Of course it's him. Who else could it be?"

"It could be a lot of people," Max said slowly. "But when you think about it, who was the one person who kept us apart for all these years? Who made sure we didn't talk to one another back then and kept the anger burning all this time?"

Spike snorted. "We did, Max. You and me. You said yourself earlier — neither of us has heard from Harvey in fifteen years, so how could he be responsible for keeping us apart?"

Max's hands went up in frustration. "He poisoned our minds, man! I can still remember the things he said about you. Terrible things. I never trusted you after that."

Spike turned to face Max. "Then why trust me now?"

"Because I'm looking you in the face and I know you wouldn't have done or said those things about me."

Spike nodded slowly. "But I did say them, Max. That's the problem."

Just then Sami Lee came to the door.

"Hon?" Max said, looking up at her.

"It's time," she said. "I'm going up to bed."

Max stood with a groan and turned to Spike. "See you in the morning."

"Yeah," Spike said without turning. "See you."

After Max and Sami Lee had gone, Spike wandered back to the parlour. He helped himself to the white powder in the bowl on the sideboard. It occurred to him that if anyone wanted to kill him, it would be the perfect place to put the poison, but he'd already indulged enough to know it was clean. At least that was one less thing to worry about.

He sat staring into space until Sandra came by to say everyone else had gone upstairs. When she left, he stopped to check the front and back doors then reluctantly followed. They were the last two to shut themselves in their rooms with a dull click of a lock.

Outside, the storm seemed to have reached some sort of climax, thrashing against the house in a fury as the wind raged and night came slowly over the island.

CHAPTER 21

Max sat up and looked at the bedside clock: 3:32 a.m. Sami Lee was snoring lightly. Her sleep mask had slipped partially off, leaving one eye visible and the other hidden, like some two-faced character from mythology. She'd wiped off her makeup before bed. Now the darkness and heavy lines around her eyes were just from age.

Max listened intently. Faraway, he thought he heard a sound like breaking glass. A minute later, there was a soft shushing that might have been the rain, but could also be someone moving around out in the hallway. He slipped quietly out of bed, trying not to disturb Sami Lee.

He opened the door a crack and listened. Silence. The hall lay in darkness.

Max hesitated. Should he go out and investigate? It was probably nothing, but then again someone could be trying to get into the house from outside.

He slipped out and stood in the shadows. The only thing he heard was the sound of an empty house coming to rest in the night. There was no one around. He headed along the hall till he reached the railing overlooking the foyer. Grasping it with both hands, he looked down to the black-and-white tiles.

A faint glow from the skylight overhead illuminated the squares. Funny, he thought, how the pattern resembled an oversized chessboard from above. He hadn't really noticed that till now. There was no movement below. He tried to recall the sound that had woken him. Could it have been a window breaking?

Softly padding feet came up behind him. He turned.

"Sorry," Max said. "Did I wake you?"

Before there was time for an answer, a pair of hands reached out and gave him a surprisingly solid shove. Max went backwards over the railing, reaching up to the skylight as though to grasp the moon or a distant star shining down on him from the far end of the universe. He didn't stop to think how the light from those stars had left their heavenly bodies centuries earlier and were now probably the last remnants of some dead planet. Also, he didn't care. Because by then his skull had cracked open as he hit the tiled floor below, landing in a neatly symmetrical pattern over half-white and half-black squares.

Sometime later, Sami Lee's screaming woke the household. Muffled sounds could be heard coming from the guest rooms as, one by one, doors opened and people emerged to see what the fuss was.

They found Sami Lee standing at the railing, looking down where Max was splayed out on the foyer tiles. A thin line of red had crept from his body and along to the window, as though it too wished to escape the house and its madness.

They all went downstairs. Sandra was already there, kneeling over the body. She felt for a pulse, but Max was dead.

It took a long time to calm Sami Lee down. When her hysterics finally stopped, Verna, Crispin, Pete, and Sandra all waited patiently as Spike addressed her.

"Tell us what happened," he said.

She explained how she'd woken as the dawn light began transforming the room and shapes emerged in the cold light of morning. Feeling beside her for Max's warmth, she found an empty space, long since cold. It wasn't unlike him to wake in the night — he'd suffered bouts of insomnia for as long as she had known him. She thought he was probably downstairs in the drawing room with the instruments, working out some musical riff or other.

She got up to check that the door was still locked. But it wasn't. She knew Max would never have left her alone with the door unlocked and she felt a rush of panic. What would make him go out without telling her? Why had he left her defenceless while she slept?

She stepped out into the hallway. There was no one else about. She listened for a sound, but heard nothing coming from anywhere in the house.

She walked to the end of the hall. If Max wasn't in the drawing room, she thought he might be in the dining room nursing a cup of coffee. Possibly he'd decided to get a head start on breakfast. She stood by the railing. The skylight showed the heavy greyness had continued. The wind had lightened a little, but the rain was still steady.

"And that's when you looked down?" Sandra asked.

Sami Lee nodded, her eyes outlined in black like a grim sorceress.

"I looked down and saw him. I knew immediately that he was dead." She choked back a sob. "Who did this?" she shrieked, looking around accusingly at all of them. "Who would kill Max?"

"We don't know for sure that anyone killed him," Crispin reminded them. "He could have become confused and fallen over the railing in the darkness. As a sight-impaired person, I live with the possibility of such danger every day."

"Yeah, right," Spike said. "Like Max would ever let that happen to him."

Verna pulled the collar of her nightgown across her chest. "I'm sorry, Sami Lee," she said. "I'm so sorry."

"I'm sure you'll understand if I say I don't believe you," Sami Lee said coldly.

"Max didn't fall over the railing," Spike said. "He was pushed. So we have to consider that either someone got inside last night or one of us did this." He looked at them meaningfully. "Did anybody hear or see anything?"

"No," Verna said.

Pete shook his head. "Me either."

"I didn't hear a thing," Sandra said. "I slept soundly for once. I mean, considering everything that's been going on it's a surprise any of us slept at all, but I was so tired I was dead to the world." Her hand went up to her mouth. "Bad choice of words — I'm sorry."

Crispin cocked his head. "I thought I heard something at one point. It almost sounded like breaking glass."

"Where did the sound come from?" Spike asked.

"From one of the guest rooms," Crispin said. "Or so I thought. I put it down to my overactive imagination. I'm sorry now I didn't get up to investigate."

"Probably good you didn't," Spike said. "It might have been you instead of Max."

Sandra interrupted. "We should check to see if the outside doors are still locked or if any of the windows are broken."

Spike stood and went first to one door and then the other. He gave each one a good rattle. "They're both locked."

"There's also the kitchen entrance," Sandra added. "It was locked yesterday after the scare with the gas and then David's death, but someone could have unlocked it."

Spike went to check. "It's still locked," he reported on his return. "And as far as I can tell, all the ground-floor windows are still intact."

Sandra nodded slowly. "So that means if Max was murdered then someone lured him out of bed and waited till he stood at the railing before pushing him over. It had to have been one of us."

A chill went round the room.

"I agree," Spike said. "We all claim we went to bed at the same time. But for some reason Max got up in the middle of the night and wandered around the house without anybody hearing him. Except someone did. And that person has to be lying. There are six of us sitting here right now and one of us is lying. One of us came to the island deliberately to kill the rest of us."

"Well, it's simple then, isn't it?" Sami Lee said scornfully. "We just have to wait till everybody's dead but that one person, then we'll have our killer."

Verna looked at her for a moment then turned away. "I'll go put coffee on for the rest of us." She paused. "Does anybody want to come and watch?"

No one answered, so Verna simply turned and went to the kitchen. A moment later, her voice reached them. It was a cross between a sigh and a moan of fear.

"Are you all right?" Sandra called out.

"Oh!" was all they heard.

Spike, Sandra, and Pete went running, leaving Sami Lee and Crispin with the body. They found Verna in the drawing room.

She shook her head. "I don't know what made me pass through this room instead of going straight to the kitchen, but when I got here —"

Her voice broke. They looked to where she was pointing at the chessboard. There were now seven pieces lying on their sides. A black king had been placed on its side along with all the others.

A small glass vase lay shattered on the floor beside the board game.

"The broken glass," Spike said. He looked at Crispin. "That's what you heard."

"But when?" Verna said. "When could someone have knocked over the chess piece?"

"It could have been any time between last night and this morning," Spike answered. *Or it could have been done by you just now*, he thought to himself.

"You mean someone killed Max and then calmly came downstairs to knock this stupid chess piece on its side?" Verna's chest heaved. She seemed on the verge of hyperventilating.

Half an hour later, the six remaining guests were seated at breakfast. Sami Lee smoked while the others ate. Every few minutes one or another of them glanced suspiciously around at the group.

"What are you looking at?" Sami Lee snapped when Verna glanced in her direction.

"Nothing," Verna said.

"Say it!" Sami Lee demanded. "You, with your need to confess everything. I can tell you're thinking something."

Verna sniffed. "All right. I was thinking how odd it was that your makeup wasn't even smeared when you got up and found Max's body. It looked freshly applied. Obviously you didn't sleep in it. How was it you had time to paint your face before coming down to find him, if you were so worried about where he was?"

Sami Lee looked as though she would explode. "Are you saying I killed Max?" she screamed. "Why would I kill him?"

"Maybe because you didn't know he'd had an affair with me and you flew into a jealous rage. Maybe you didn't know he used to fuck me and let me suck his cock."

Sami Lee laughed scornfully. "You're pathetic. A lot of people sucked Max's cock."

Verna's chin jutted in the air. "Maybe you were worried he'd leave you for me. I'm a lot better-looking than you. You're a dried-up old hag."

"You stupid hermaphrodite!" Sami Lee reached across the table to slap her, but Verna sat back out of reach.

"I'm not a hermaphrodite!"

"This is not very constructive," Crispin's voice warned. "This is probably exactly what someone wants to happen here. We've got to think with the mentality of this killer, who would be more than happy to have us set ourselves one against the other. My guess is that's just what he or she is hoping will happen."

"Crispin's right," Spike said. "We can't afford to fall into that trap. We've got to concentrate on staying alive until someone comes to rescue us."

"And when will that be?" Sami Lee glared at them.

"There's no way of knowing," Crispin answered. "But eventually someone's got to come by."

"But that's the brilliance of it, isn't it?" Verna said. "Don't you see? This is an exclusive retreat. There's no mail delivery or food drop-off. More likely than not, no one ever comes here."

She slumped in her seat.

Crispin shook his head. "Soon enough someone is going to realize that none of us have been in touch for days and start a search. It will happen." He paused before repeating himself in a softer voice. "It will happen. I know it will. In the meantime, once the weather clears up the sailboats will start to come by. We'll flag one down. We could even start a fire once this rain stops."

"By then we'll all be dead," said Sami Lee. She got up and went to the front door. She unfastened the lock and stepped out into the rain.

"You probably shouldn't go out and wander around," Pete told her. "Whoever it is might try something when you're alone."

"Who fucking cares?" she said, and slammed the door behind her.

Verna looked at Spike. "Shouldn't someone follow her? She's not safe."

Sandra spoke up. "If we try to follow her, she'll think she's being stalked. I wouldn't."

"Or maybe she feels safe because she knows who did this," Spike said. "She could have pushed Max over the railing then gone back to bed and gotten up later and claimed she'd been asleep the whole time."

"Why would she do that?" Pete asked.

"Maybe Verna's right," Sandra said with a stricken look. "Maybe she was jealous."

They looked around at one another.

"Between you and me," Spike said, "I've always hated the bitch. I never trusted her. I thought she was capable of anything. She was far worse for the group than Harvey. It was Sami Lee who turned Max against the rest of us."

"Having bad feelings toward someone is never a good reason for believing them capable of committing murder," Crispin's rational voice spoke up. "She's peevish and hard to get along with, but let's not write her off as a killer just because of those qualities."

"Then who do you think it is, sport?"

A grim smile played over Crispin's mouth. "In my estimation, it could just as easily be you or Sandra or Pete or even me." He paused to let this sink in. "Let's not make silly insinuations without something to back up our suspicions. We'll all be raving lunatics before the day's out if we start suspecting everybody."

Spike stared at him. "Then what do you suggest?"

"I suggest we all go upstairs and get dressed and carry on with our daily activities. Surely I'm not the only one with things that need attending to? Or did you want to carry out another search of the island and risk catching pneumonia? I don't think there were any antibiotics in that medicine kit."

"No, there weren't," Sandra confirmed.

"Well, there we go then. Let's all just concentrate on staying alive and healthy. This can't go on for much longer."

CHAPTER 22

Up in his room, Pete sat on his bed and tried to think. The silence in his head was deafening. The Voice hadn't spoken all morning. He remembered distinctly the first time he heard it. It was a few weeks prior to the trial, during the build-up of hysteria over the death of the girl, Zerin Ames. At first he wasn't sure whose voice he was hearing that morning as he stood staring at his haggard face in the bathroom mirror. He'd been on a week-long heroin bender. Then suddenly he heard it loud and clear. It told him to keep calm and get into a methadone clinic. If he did, it promised, the case would go well for him and the other band members.

Pete hadn't paid much attention at the time. His mind was too distracted to think. But each day as he woke it was there speaking to him, insisting he listen and do as it said. Like following a yellow brick road. And so he finally did. The very next day, he learned the charges against the band had been dropped.

The Voice came and went. It seemed to be around most whenever he needed a friend. And that was what it seemed to be, for the most part. A bossy friend, but a friend nonetheless. Like a distant conscience. At first, Pete hadn't fully trusted it, but as time wore on he realized it never intended harm. He grew to accept that it was always there with him, unheard by anyone else.

He never knew when it would speak. At times when the Voice got too insistent, Pete would try to drown it out with alcohol. Even good friends needed to learn when to back off. The tactic was effective at first, but alcohol soon became a constant. Only after a while it wasn't always so effective at keeping the Voice out. Somehow, it knew when to come looking for him. And it always found him. These days, it came through in his dreams if he managed to block it out during his waking life.

Pete sat and thought about the others in the house. Over the past few days, he'd been quietly observing their movements and waiting to see what they would do next. He felt reasonably sure the Voice knew who the murderer was, and that it would eventually reveal the secret to him. For now, it was biding its time. He could never prompt it to speak until it was ready. That's just how the Voice was.

Pete was vigilant and tried hard to listen whenever it spoke to him. It knew things, he realized, and therefore it had to be listened to when it spoke. The only thing he didn't trust, and didn't like, were the blackouts. They could come and go without warning, catching him off guard. Sometimes the Voice warned him when they were coming. When they did, he would crawl off to bed and wake hours or sometimes even days later without remembering a thing. There were no dreams during these blackouts, just a never-ending darkness that pulled him into its depths and kept him unconscious. He often wondered why the Voice never spoke to him then, but the Voice did what the Voice wanted to do. It wasn't his place to ask why.

Spike passed his doorway. He paused, looking in at Pete, who sat mumbling to himself on his bed. Sometimes he wondered what went on in his head. It had to be a strange world in there. Still, he refused to believe that Pete was dangerous.

Spike waved at him and continued down the hall to Max and Sami Lee's room. He stood before the green door a moment then let himself in. He stood looking down at Max's body. Max looked more like he was asleep than anything. Spike was half convinced he would see a slightly imperceptible rise in Max's chest as he breathed in and out. *You old faker,* he wanted to say.

But nothing happened. Spike just stood there looking down at his friend's lifeless body. *So this is it*, he told himself. *Endgame. Checkmate. I've won, buddy. Who would have thought after all these years it would be me to survive and not you? Too bad for you, Max. But as you see, I've clearly emerged the winner. And when I leave here tomorrow, or maybe the next day, this will all be in the past. But I'll make you a promise: I'll sign those contracts to finish the recording. I'll finish it for both of us. It will be our epitaph.*

He crept back out of the room and headed downstairs.

The day wore on. Sami Lee returned, drenched, and went upstairs without speaking to anyone. Most of the others stayed holed up in their bedrooms, but Spike preferred to sit in the drawing room staring at the chessboard that seemed to rearrange itself of its own accord. In fact, there was something different about it now, but try as he might, he couldn't bring to mind what it was.

He looked over at the stage with its setup of instruments that would never be played. The thought of finishing *Endgame* stayed with him. He and Pete could finish the tracks they recorded before the group split up. Max's part was pretty much finished. And now that Max was dead, the rivalry between them could be laid to rest forever. It seemed appropriate. The album would serve as some sort of tribute, however belated, to Max and Kent. Yes, when he got off the island and returned home, he would do it for his late bandmates.

In the other room, the bowls of goodies beckoned. He traipsed out to the parlour. It was a toss-up between the grass and the white powder. The powder won out. He took one sniff and then another. This was the most dope he'd done in years. He'd have to pull back soon or he'd be looking at another full-fledged addiction. He tried to recall the next verse for the "Twelve Days of Shagging." Then it came to him: "seven crystals shining." But he'd been using the stuff since he arrived.

Spike went back to the drawing room and relaxed in his chair. Despite the chemicals he'd put up his nose, he was still able to make out the smell of something burning. It was foul, like a soup pot left too long on the stove. No matter. He could feel sleep coming at last. His high was finally winding down. It was about time. He hadn't slept for days. Of course, he hadn't told anyone that he'd been awake when Max was killed. That would have been too much information for them. Obvious conclusions would have been drawn and the suspicion set to fall on him.

He'd just drifted off when he felt a prick in his neck like the sting of a bee. He tried to sit up, but his physical reactions had already begun to fail. His eyelids drooped. His muscles stopped fighting. Somewhere in the distance, he heard a scream. It was his last conscious sensation before everything went black forever.

Upstairs, everyone rushed to the aid of the screamer. Sami Lee stood in her room breathing tensely. She clutched her head with both hands while the others congregated in the hall.

"I'm going to scream again if someone doesn't get rid of it," Sami Lee said.

Verna looked around, but could see nothing out of order except for Max's body.

"What is it?" she asked.

"The chess piece!" Sami Lee replied angrily. "Who left it there?"

There, on Max's chest where the covers had been pulled back, lay a small black king.

Verna looked around with an accusing stare. "Someone," she said, "has a very sick sense of humour."

"Indeed, someone has a rather diabolical sense of humour," Crispin agreed, standing behind her in the doorway. "Not to put too fine a point on it."

Pete showed up at that moment. "What's happened?"

"Look," Sandra said, pointing out the offending piece.

"Where were you just now, Pete?" Sami Lee demanded in an accusing tone.

"I was in my room — trying to sleep," Pete replied. "It took me a while to break out of the fog I was in."

"Where's Spike?" Verna asked suddenly.

Everyone looked around. Spike was not among them.

"Maybe he went outside," Pete said. "He's probably sick of being cooped up in here for so long."

"I think we should look for him, in any case," Crispin said.

Verna went out into the hallway. "Spike?" she cried out.

An ominous silence came from the rest of the house in answer to her call. There was also a terrible odour coming from downstairs, as though something had died and been set on fire.

"I don't like this," Verna said. "Will someone please come downstairs with me to check?"

"I'll come with you," Sandra said.

Together they made their way down to the main floor. They looked outside on the porch first, thinking Spike might be sitting out there smoking a joint. Next they peeked into the kitchen where a small dish of ashes seemed to be responsible for the burning smell.

"What is that vile concoction?" Verna asked.

"I don't know," Sandra said, tossing it in the garbage. "It looks like someone was cooking something and left it to burn."

When they entered the drawing room, Verna saw Spike's green hair sticking up over top of the chair as he sat with his back to them.

"Spike!" Verna said. "You gave us quite a start."

There was no movement as they approached.

"He's sleeping," Verna said.

"I don't know," Sandra said nervously.

Spike's eyes were closed and his hands clasped peacefully on his lap, as though clutched in prayer. White powder stained his shirt front. If it hadn't been for the hypodermic plunged into his neck, they might have thought him asleep. Sandra felt his wrist for a pulse and shook her head.

"This just happened," she said. "His body is still warm. While we were all upstairs, he was down here dying."

Verna began to gasp. "But how? We were all upstairs together!"

Sandra looked at her coldly. "We thought we were all upstairs, but Pete took a little longer to get there than the rest of us, didn't he?"

"Oh, no!" Verna cried, shaking her head. "It can't be. It can't be."

Sandra grabbed her wrist in a grip that was hard enough to hurt. "It's got to be! Don't you see?"

Verna just stood there shaking her head. "I can't believe it. I can't believe it's any of us, really. I just can't."

"Don't panic," Sandra said. "You've got to keep calm."

Verna looked around the room. "Oh my god!" she gasped.

Yet another chess piece had been toppled. Now the white king lay on its side, leaving two queens, a bishop, a knight, and a pawn.

Sandra turned her head in the direction of the stairs where footsteps could be heard approaching.

"Is everything okay down there?" they heard Pete call out.

CHAPTER 23

Outside, the rain was torrential. The wind had revived and was approaching gale force. Storms in the Sound were known for their fierce gusts as well as their record-breaking precipitation, but this one seemed to be trying for a new record. Inside, the remaining five guests were beset by storms of their own. Spike's body was carried upstairs and laid out in his bedroom. Sandra suggested putting the two former band members together in the same room so Sami Lee could sleep alone in Spike's room, but she refused.

"I'm staying with Max," she exclaimed with a shake of the head. "I won't leave him."

"But what happens …?" Sandra began, but stopped herself from saying what she was thinking.

Sami Lee turned a baleful eye on her. "What happens when the body rots and starts to stink so much I can't stand it? I'll worry about that, not you."

"Of course. My apologies," Sandra said, and headed for the hallway.

"Wait." It was Crispin.

Sandra turned back.

"I think it goes without saying that we've broken the golden rule far too many times. We must all stick together from now on," Crispin admonished roughly. "We can't afford to wander off on our own."

Sami Lee looked at him long and hard. "Are you going to come with me when I need to take a piss?"

"Perhaps one of the ladies will go with you instead," he said, all the fight gone from his voice.

Sami Lee took a hard look at Verna and then at Sandra. "I only see one other 'lady' in the room besides me," she said. "I'll take my chances on my own."

"I don't need anyone following me around, either," Pete spat out. "From now on, I don't trust anybody. Not a single one of you!"

"As you wish," said Crispin. "I merely suggest it for the good of all …"

"Fuck you and your 'good of all,'" Sami Lee sneered. "A lot of good it's done any of us so far. If we'd all stayed far apart, probably none of this would have happened. It's sticking together that's getting us killed."

"Surely you don't believe that," Sandra said softly. "We've all been trying to look after one another."

"Well, if that's true, somebody isn't doing a very good job of it," Sami Lee said.

"I will suggest one other thing then," Crispin told them. "When we are alone in our rooms, I suggest that if anyone wants to alert the others, he or she should knock three times either on the heating vents or on everyone's door if we leave. That way, we will know that each of us has been alerted."

The afternoon whiled away. Each of the guests stayed in his or her room. At three o'clock, there came three gentle knocks on each of their doors. It was Crispin, calling a conference to declare that he needed to eat to keep his blood sugar levels stable.

"The last thing I want to think about is food," Sami Lee said, glaring at him when she opened the door.

"I'm sorry if I appear callous," he said, "but my dietary needs are fairly important. I would appreciate it if at least one of you would come to the kitchen with me."

"I'm hungry, too," Pete said. "Maybe we should all eat something."

Sami Lee looked at Pete. "At a time like this? Crispin needs to eat because he's sick. What's your excuse?"

Pete glared at her. "Why don't you shut the fuck up? I think we should all go downstairs together, even if we don't eat."

"Fine," Sami Lee said. "Let's go downstairs so you can fill your gullet."

They all left together and sat gloomily in the dining room. Sami Lee smoked while the others passed a can opener, taking turns till they had opened four cans of tuna. Next they retrieved a loaf of white bread from the freezer, thawing the slices individually in the toaster.

"I'm not really hungry," said Verna, turning away from the food when it was finally set before her.

"Me either," Sami Lee said. "The rest of you can eat, if you have the stomach for it."

"Of course, you realize any of this could have been doctored with poison before we even got here," Sandra said, glancing in distaste at the bread on the table.

Pete looked up and said scornfully, "Fuck it. Gotta keep my strength up." He grabbed two slices of toast. "At least I won't die hungry."

"You think this is funny?" Sami Lee demanded.

"Yeah. I think it's a big fucking joke, Sami Lee. How about you?"

Her mouth tensed as she watched him. "I think you're getting a sadistic little kick out of this, you bastard."

"Think what you like, bitch," he told her, munching on the toast.

Smile, the Voice told him. *Show the cunt you don't care what she thinks.*

He bared his teeth at her.

"You look like a dog," she said. "A fucking rabid dog."

"And you look like a goddamn vampire, so shut up. Let me eat my fucking meal in peace."

Pete turned away from the table and chewed while looking out at the rain beating against the windowpane. *Stupid cow*, he thought. *Now that Max isn't here, I'll smash her in the face if she doesn't shut her mouth.*

Once he'd finished eating, Crispin stood and cocked his head at the room. "Thank you all for coming down with me. I am going to take some bread and cheese upstairs with me to my room," he said. "I doubt whether I'll be back down for supper."

He waited, but no one offered to accompany him.

"If I run into any trouble, I shall call out. I hope at least one of you will be so good as to come to my aid."

Having made his request, he turned and headed up the stairs.

Sandra stood and cleared the dishes, taking them out to the kitchen. She was back in a moment and looked around at the others.

"I'm not doing any dishes without help. Perhaps we can all clean up later. I should probably be going back to my room, too," she said. "I doubt that my company is doing much to cheer anyone here, so I can leave feeling relatively assured that I won't be missed."

Before she could leave the room, however, Crispin returned and stood in the doorway. He looked as though he were unable to speak.

"What's up?" Pete asked him. "I thought you said you weren't coming back."

"Are you okay?" Sandra asked.

Crispin shook his head and swallowed. "I think someone has just been in my room."

"What?" Sami Lee cried.

"My laptop is missing," he said. "It's possible I may have misplaced it in all the confusion, but I don't think so."

"But that's impossible," Verna said. "We've all been here the entire time. Haven't we?" She looked around for confirmation.

"That's right," said Sandra. "None of us left the room since we found Spike. The three of you arrived downstairs together."

"I know that …" Crispin began.

"How would someone get in your room?" Sandra interrupted.

"I may have left the room unlocked when we came downstairs. In fact, I'm sure I did."

"There has to be someone else in the house," Verna said. "There has to be!"

"How could there be?" said Pete.

"I suggest we look again, one room at a time," Crispin said. "I can't think of any other way to be sure."

Verna and Sandra each retrieved their respective keys, unlocking the cupboard over the fridge. The master key ring lay where they had left it. They next went together up to Crispin's room and looked for his laptop. A thorough search revealed nothing.

"Why would someone want your laptop? What's on it?" Sandra asked him.

Crispin's voice was hesitant. "The tapes," he said. "I've been transcribing them night after night when everyone else has gone to bed. Perhaps someone said something they don't want confirmed about their actions the night of Zerin Ames's death."

"That could be just about anybody," Sami Lee said scornfully.

"In any case," Crispin continued, "at least they don't have the original recordings. I've kept those with me at all times."

"Then you better hope they don't come back and kill you for them," Sami Lee said.

One by one, they searched the rooms. It was difficult not to look at the bodies laid out on their beds. Noni's and Janice's rooms had already begun to be tainted by a slight thickening of the air. They discussed leaving the windows open, but agreed that would only make it easier for anyone outside trying to get into the house.

"Even up here on the third floor?" Verna asked skeptically.

Crispin nodded. "Even here. Whoever is behind this is a diabolical killer who will probably stop at nothing. We'd just be leaving ourselves open to attack."

In the end, it was agreed the doors and windows would remain locked. After searching upstairs, the group continued downstairs. There was no sign of the laptop or anything suggestive of a forced entry.

At one point, Crispin pulled Sandra aside. "I didn't want to say anything to the others, but my entire insulin supply is in that laptop bag. Do you have any in your medical kit, in case I absolutely need it?"

"Yes, but ..." She left the sentence unfinished.

"But do I really want to chance it? Is that what you're thinking?"

"Yes," she said softly. "That's it."

"We'll cross that bridge when we come to it."

When the search was over, the master key ring was returned to its hiding place.

That night, once again, all doors were locked as the five remaining guests slept an unquiet sleep. No one stirred; no sounds were heard in the corridors. No secret knocks were enacted during what seemed like an endless night.

CHAPTER 24

There was no lessening of the rain overnight, but by morning the wind had died down a little. It held a promise for calmer seas on the morrow. Breakfast itself was a quiet affair, with surreptitious glances passed back and forth among the five remaining guests.

Sandra thought Crispin appeared wan and listless when he came down the stairs, but he made no complaints. The others were simply too preoccupied to notice.

"Coffee?" she asked him.

"No, thank you," he replied. He cocked his head to the room, as though to ascertain how many people were in his company. "I know it's difficult to say these things, but it all points to one conclusion: the killer is one of us. It might help if we talk about probabilities here. Who is likeliest to have done this? Who has the strongest motive? Revenge? Hatred? Betrayal?"

His blind eyes turned toward them one by one.

"Yes, all of the above, but for what purpose?" Verna said. "A young woman died. It's sad, but why go to all this effort for revenge?"

"Yes," Crispin said. "That's just it. Who is most likely to get upset about it to such a degree that they would seek revenge? A boyfriend? A lover? Family member?"

There was no answer.

"Again, you would think it could be all of the above, yes?" he continued. "So who knew the girl personally? Any of us?"

Everyone seemed to be avoiding his blind, questioning stare.

Verna sighed. "I never met her before the night of the party. You don't have to believe me, but it's true."

Crispin nodded. "If we accept that this is the truth, then you clearly had no motive for wanting to see her dead. Yet you made the suggestion not to allow the emergency call to be made."

Verna stifled a gasp. She shook her head. "I told you. I didn't want the police to get involved so I … I …"

They waited while she struggled to speak.

"Someone picked up the phone to dial emergency," Verna continued. "I just advised them not to make the call."

"You pulled the phone out of Spike's hands," Sami Lee corrected her. "That's what I remember."

Verna turned her head away. "Yes," she said in a whispery voice. "I stopped the call."

"Then you're in the clear," Crispin said. "If you contributed to her death, you can't want revenge on anybody else for what happened," he concluded. "What about a nurse? Someone sworn to saving human life? Could a nurse take exception to the awful things that went on and want revenge for what she saw as the senseless destruction of one of her patients?"

They all looked to Sandra, who shook her head. "After a while, you don't think that way. It's sad, but it happens. Especially with drug abuse. You can't save everyone. But that's not the reason I'm here. I think the killer knows this."

The others waited for her to continue.

Sandra looked down. "Newt — David Merton — and I used to know one another back then. I supplied him with the medication he used to make his drug cocktails. I stole from the hospital pharmacy," she said, her voice reduced almost to a whisper. "'Party martinis,' he called them. Whatever I could get my hands on that might not be missed, I passed along. Free samples. Anything past the expiry date. I guess he made a mistake with his combinations and it turned lethal. At least, it was lethal for Zerin Ames. If she'd got help in time we could have done something, but it was a tragic chain of events that went from bad to worse."

Crispin's hand dropped to the table with a thud. They turned to look at him. His head hung back. His eyelids fluttered, revealing those eerie blue portals. His breath came in gasps.

Sandra ran to him.

"It's my insulin," he said.

"I'll get the medicine kit," she said calmly. She looked at the others. "Keep him comfortable. I won't be a minute."

She rushed to her room and quickly returned with the kit. They all watched anxiously as she stabbed the tiny bottle with a needle tip and drew a dropper of liquid into the cavity.

She looked intently at Crispin. "Do you really want me to do this?"

"I haven't any choice," he gasped.

"We could risk waiting to see if anyone shows up this morning."

"I might be in a coma by then. Come on, let's do it."

She rolled Crispin's sleeve back and jabbed the needle deep into a vein, injecting the entire dosage. Crispin sighed and relaxed. At first, nothing happened. The others breathed with relief. Suddenly, a spasm shook Crispin's body. His face registered extreme agony. A cry that sounded like the howl of a wounded animal came from the depths of his being. He shook and convulsed as the others tried to hold him down. Then, almost as quickly as it began, it was over. He lay still.

"You've killed him," Verna said in horror, looking down at his unmoving body.

Sandra stared at the syringe in her shaking hand. "I can't

have," she said. "It was just insulin."

"How do you know?" Pete asked. "It could have been any-thing in that bottle."

Sandra dropped the needle onto the floor where it rolled to one side. Tears fell from her eyes.

"My god…!"

"It's not your fault," Sami Lee said. "We were set up from the beginning. Whoever did this is a sick, sadistic bastard. If I find out which one of you it is …"

She left the threat unfinished. Three faces stared at her in bewilderment.

"It's not me," cried Verna. "It's not!"

"Nor me," Sandra said, weeping softly.

"I wouldn't harm a fly," Pete said, his head hanging down. "Or a human being."

"Well, then, that makes four of us. But someone here is lying," Sami Lee told them. "And I know it isn't me."

Sandra looked at Crispin's tape recorder where he'd left it on the table. "He thought someone wanted the information he had on this," she said, fingering the device.

"You mean our confessions," Sami Lee reminded them, star-ing at it. "Yes, maybe."

She reached across the table and pulled it toward her. "I'm in charge of this from now on. If anything else happens before help comes, I'm going to record it. So be warned that anything you say from now on will end up on this machine."

She stood and left the room, taking the recorder with her.

"Who does she think she is?" Verna asked, looking at Sandra and Pete.

"I've been wondering that myself for the past twenty years," Pete said.

CHAPTER 25

Pete and Sandra carried Crispin upstairs. Verna was filled with trepidation as she unlocked the room beside hers and they brought him in, laying him out as though on a funeral bier like all the others.

"I suppose he should be in here and not somewhere else," Verna said, mostly to herself. She shivered. "I just wish we could put him in someone else's room."

"This was his room," Sami Lee said coldly. "He's staying here."

They left the room and locked it behind them.

"The dead don't walk," Sami Lee said to Verna. "You won't have to worry that he'll come into your room and murder you next."

"So what do we do now?" Pete asked. "Sit around all day watching one another as we go crazy, or do we just lock ourselves in our rooms and stay there till help comes?"

"I suggest we try to make a fire and send up a smoke signal," Sami Lee said. "I for one don't intend to sit here and wait to be killed."

Without Max to look after her, she'd become a more dominant personality. Somehow, she seemed to have found an inner resolve.

In the end, it was agreed they would light a fire on the cliff facing the mainland. The results were dismal at best. There was little hope anyone would even be looking for smoke signals on a small island in the middle of a rainstorm. After half an hour, they gave up and returned to the house.

"How long can this fucking rain go on?" Sami Lee said, shaking her fist at the sky.

At noon, they convened in the dining room and had another meal of canned tuna. The bread had run out and no one wanted to cook. The kettle was filled under everyone's watchful eye. When the whistle blew, each of the four chose a tea bag and inserted it into a cup as the water was poured. The fridge had remained unplugged so no one bothered with milk.

The scene was repeated again at six o'clock for supper. In the middle of the meal the power went off, plunging them in darkness.

"Fucking power corporation," Sami Lee said.

"We better check the fuses," Sandra told them. "But we'll do it together."

It was agreed they would all go down to the electrical room, one after another, holding a single flashlight. Pete stumbled on the stairs and broke the chain. There was a moment of panic before the line was resumed as, hand in hand, they moved forward and found the switch breakers. Just as they opened the panel, the power suddenly came on again. They stumbled back upstairs, nervous and edgy.

It was then Pete realized he hadn't checked the chess board after Crispin's death. True to form, he found the black bishop tipped over on its side. *Eight poisoned needles*, mocked the Voice. Pete shivered and shut the door to the drawing room without telling the others.

Supper was soon over and the dishes washed jointly. They retired to their rooms by eight. It was agreed that no one needed to emerge before morning, so no secret knock was prearranged.

Sandra lay in bed envisioning over and over again the scene in which she asked Crispin if he wanted to trust the insulin. She saw him nod, knowing there really was no choice. If she didn't give it to him, he would die. But he died anyway. The look of agony on his face, the twisted lips and bulging eyes were forever burned into her memory. No matter how long she lived, she would never forget that sight.

She'd seen many troubling things, but nothing quite as awful as that. Before, when she'd concocted the compounds to put people out of their misery, they had simply and peacefully gone off to sleep, never to awaken. But this was different. This was a man who still wanted very much to live. As far as she was concerned, there was no reason anyone should want to see him die that way.

Pete, too, lay in bed. He was waiting for the Voice to make itself known, but nothing came in the hours he lay there. Eventually, he drifted off into an uneasy sleep where he found himself examining an urn in a garden. The urn lay on its side. With a great effort, he managed to set it upright, but as he did he saw it was no longer an urn but a giant chess piece. A black knight. As he stood and brushed off his hands, he heard an unearthly buzzing. He watched as a swarm of wasps emerged from the knight's mouth. Hundreds of them.

He held his breath and kept very still as they began to zoom around, lighting on his clothes and in his hair. Then, sensing he wasn't what they were looking for, the wasps turned as one and flew off in another direction.

Sami Lee lay awake trying to piece together the strange chain of events that brought them to Shark Island. First had been Harvey's letter turning up suddenly and Max shouting for joy upon reading the news. Then Pete called asking to join them. How could they have known the terrible things that awaited them? On the other hand, it was fitting for a star to go out in a blaze of glory rather than fade away. It wasn't right for a legend like Max to end up old and destitute. Stars had to die young in order to stay immortal, otherwise what was the point of being a star? Stars didn't fade. They crashed and burned and exploded. Their legends demanded it. So Max had fulfilled his destiny by dying here on Shark Island.

Verna, too, lay awake, thinking of that awful night of the party twenty years ago. She could still see herself as Werner, how he seemed to speak those words as if he'd been prompted: "Don't call 911. Don't get the police involved or we're all screwed!"

Until then, no one had paid much attention to Werner, but suddenly it was as if he were in command. Amazingly, no one contested him when he took the phone from Spike's hand.

"What do we do then?" Spike asked.

"Send her in a taxi," Sami Lee had said.

Werner argued, "But then they'll know where she was picked up and they'll come looking for us." He felt very much in control, as if he had thought this all out beforehand.

"We'll take her outside and meet the taxi on the corner," Max said.

And so Zerin Ames's fate had been decided for the convenience of everyone else.

Later the story was concocted that she'd been taken to the taxi by two unknown men, friends of Zerin's who left the party with her and were never seen again. At the trial, Newt Merton pleaded no contest on the advice of Noni Embrem and went to jail. And, but for fifty thousand dollars in cash, he might have told the truth about everyone else's involvement. But he didn't.

End of story.

It was while she was reliving these terrible memories that Verna heard a scratching sound coming from the roof. She sat up in bed and looked around, but saw nothing in the darkness. She listened carefully. The scratching stopped. Now there was another sound in the room. A faint buzzing. And suddenly, Verna knew how she would die.

None of the others could remember when they eventually drifted off to a sleep disturbed by dark happenings, but they all recalled clearly what woke them: a scream in the night. In the confusion that followed, no one was willing to emerge from his or her room without the secret knock, but eventually Sami Lee came out, followed by Pete and Sandra. They convened in front of Verna's door where they could hear her whimpering inside, but nothing more.

"Open it," Sami Lee commanded.

"We can't. Verna's got the other key to the cupboard," Sandra said. "Mine opens the case the master key ring is in. Without Verna's key, I can't open the cupboard."

"Then break the fucking lock on the cupboard," Sami Lee told them.

Pete ran downstairs where they heard him bashing away at the cupboard. Eventually, he returned bearing the key ring. They opened Verna's room, but by then all sound had ceased.

"Careful," Sandra said. "Someone could be hiding in here."

She flicked the light on. There was no one else in the room.

Verna lay spread-eagled on the bed, naked. In her effort to escape, she'd shed her cotton nightie. Her body was covered in red welts, as though she'd been kissed all over. Her bee-stung lips were still proudly full and red. A few of the wasps were still buzzing around. Others lay dying or dead on the bedspread. On the floor beneath the window lay a large papery wasps' nest.

They spent a few minutes knocking down the rest of the flying insects before stamping on them and beating them to death.

Sami Lee looked around. "How did they get in here?"

Indeed, there was no obvious way in which the wasps might have entered the room. The curtains were pulled back, but the window was bolted from inside.

"It's impossible," Sandra said.

Check! said the Voice.

"Stop it," Pete screamed, clutching his head. "Stop playing this game!"

Sami Lee and Sandra stared at him.

"What's going on?" Sandra said.

"It won't stop," Pete said, with a deranged look on his face. "It's the Voice. It keeps telling me to look at the chessboard, but I won't go down there anymore. Why won't it leave me alone?"

"Calm down, Pete," Sami Lee commanded.

The Voice did not speak again. Pete quieted himself after a few minutes while Sami Lee and Sandra checked to make sure Verna was no longer alive.

"I was sure it was her," he said, clutching his head as though he feared the wasps might swarm him next.

"Well, clearly it wasn't," Sami Lee said.

"What now?" Sandra asked, looking fearfully around.

Sami Lee gazed at her coldly. "I suggest we all go back to bed and lock our doors and stay there until morning."

"But how will we know we're safe?" Sandra demanded. "Verna was locked in her room and the killer still got to her."

Sami Lee nodded. "We will each go downstairs to the kitchen and bring a knife into our room with us. It's the only way to be sure. Agreed?"

The other two nodded.

Together, they tromped down to the kitchen and waited while each selected a weapon, then went warily back up the stairs, trying not to think about the fact that they were all now armed. One by one, they went into their rooms and locked their doors behind them.

It's Pete, thought Sami Lee. *It's this crazy Voice he keeps hearing that tells him to kill us. Maybe he doesn't even know he's doing it, like some sort of sadistic psycho who turns into a killing machine when his alter ego takes over.*

It's Sami Lee, Sandra thought. *I know Pete sounds crazy, but he's not really capable of doing anyone any harm. Not when you come down to it. He's just a neurotic. Or maybe I'm deluding myself.*

Fucking women, Pete thought. *It could be either of them. I've always had to watch myself around women. First they steal your money, then they stab you in the back and walk out on you.*

It could be both of them, the Voice said.

Pete was startled. *Yes*, he thought. *They're probably in it together.* He clutched the handle of his knife and held it tightly. *If they try to get in here, they'll get what they deserve.*

CHAPTER 26

The three remaining guests woke simultaneously. Sandra lay in bed, not moving. Sami Lee got up and went into her bathroom, staring hard at the bathtub. She'd thought for a long time, as she lay awake, about what she was going to do today. She could wait no longer. She brushed her teeth and washed her face and grimaced at herself in the mirror. She'd once been beautiful, but that was years ago — before the drugs and the parties and the emotional abuse that living with Max had wrought.

She'd known from the start she could never have him completely. That knowledge had done terrible things to her mind. She hated each and every one of the others who had tried to steal him from her, both men and women. At one point, she'd vowed to take revenge on them all. That was a long time ago. But it had cost her. It aged her and warped her mind till she feared and hated everything that threatened to come between her and Max. So why had she stayed with him all those years? Maybe because after all was said and done, she knew he loved her. Though she had long since stopped loving him. That was the sad part. Now she had nothing left.

Till now. She smiled to herself. Yes, today was the day. She dressed and got ready for what she knew would be the final day of this long, unending nightmare that had been her life for the past twenty years.

At eight, the signal was given: three knocks on the heating vent just below ceiling level. It travelled from room to room, as Crispin had said it would on that first horrific afternoon when they knew for sure that the killer was among them.

One at a time, three doors were unlocked and cautiously opened. Three wary faces peered into the hall and breathed a sigh of relief on seeing their fellow inmates, though it was tempered with the sure knowledge that one of them intended harm toward the other two. If only — if only they could be sure which one. But that, of course, was an impossibility.

For once, Pete's Voice had been wrong. There were no changes made to the chessboard when he went downstairs and looked it over.

"Nine wasps a-stinging." Pete reached out a finger and tipped over the white queen, leaving three remaining pieces — a queen, a knight, and a pawn — upright on the board.

The other two watched him.

He turned to them. "I know what you're thinking," he said. "But it wasn't me."

"Don't touch that board again," Sami Lee said.

They'd been sitting at the table for a while before it registered that the rain had stopped. The sky was overcast with huge, woolly grey clouds moved about by the wind, but there was a calm in the air that hadn't been there when they went to their rooms the previous night.

"The fire," Sandra said. "We can build it today. Someone will come."

"Yes," Sami Lee said. "Let's do it."

They ate quickly then went to the cliffs and began searching for firewood. Everything they found was drenched. In the distance, a fishing trawler went by. They all shouted and waved, but it took no notice.

"This is nuts," Sandra told the others. "There's plenty to burn in the house. I'm going to get something before the boat gets away."

"We'll come with you," Sami Lee said.

"No," Sandra said. "You and Pete stay here and keep waving. I'm faster on my own."

She dashed off. Sami Lee looked over at Pete, who glared back at her. She waited.

"You know, don't you?" he asked.

"What do I know? About what you did to Zerin Ames at that party or what you're going to try to do to me?"

He held up his hands. "I swear it's not me, Sami Lee."

"Well, I know it's not me, either, so that makes us even on that score, at least."

"Then we agree it's Sandra?"

"Or maybe it's the Voice, Pete. Did you ever think it's the Voice making you do things? Maybe that's why you black out and come to again without any memory of what you've done."

Pete shook his head. "It's not me. I wish she would hurry up and get back here." He looked over his shoulder, but Sandra was already out of sight.

Sandra paused to look up at the house as she approached. The sky was grey and the sea restless, but it was clear the worst was past. Here and there, sunlight shone through the clouds over the water. With any luck, other boats would appear in the morning or later in the afternoon at the latest.

She took a deep breath and went up to the front door. *It's just an empty house*, she told herself. *Even if it's one of them, they're back there and I'm here alone. You can't get hurt when you're alone.* That was when a strange thought occurred to her, but she pushed it to the back of her mind, shaking it off as nonsense.

Sandra turned the knob. They'd neglected to lock the door when they left. No matter. She went in and looked around to see what would make easy material for burning. As she gathered a few wooden implements and grabbed some old magazines, she felt a sudden shiver, as though she wasn't alone. She turned and looked over her shoulder. The strange thought she'd had earlier would not leave her.

Fifteen minutes passed, then a half hour as Sami Lee and Pete waited for Sandra to come back.

"She's taking too long," Pete said. "We'd better go look for her. Who knows what she might be up to. She could have a gun hidden somewhere."

"I don't want to go back in that house," Sami Lee said.

"Fine, then I'll go alone," Pete said. "Do whatever the fuck you like, Sami Lee, but I'm going to find out what she's up to."

He turned and started to walk toward the house. Sami Lee trailed after him.

"Don't go," she said. "Pete — stop!"

But Pete continued on up to the house. The front door had been left ajar.

"Sandra?" he called out.

There was no answer. Pete went up the steps and looked inside. Steeling his courage, he went in. When he came out again, Sami Lee stood watching him.

"Did you find her?" Sami Lee asked.

Pete nodded.

"And …?"

"She'd dead."

"How can she be …?"

"She was tucked in her bed. There are purple finger marks on her neck."

"Ten stranglers strangling," Sami Lee said.

She turned and marched away.

"Where are you going?" Pete called out, watching the witchy mass of hair flying over her shoulders.

"As far away from you and this house as possible."

"But it can't have been either of us," Pete said. "We were both at the cliffs."

Sami Lee whirled and angrily confronted him. "So you say! So you say, Pete, but how do I know you didn't kill her? Or maybe she's not even dead! Maybe the two of you are waiting for me to go back inside the house so you can both kill me!" She turned and marched down to the cove. Standing on the shore, she desperately scanned the waves for signs of a boat.

Pete stomped after her and grabbed her arm, pulling her violently around to face him. "I didn't do this! You know I didn't!"

"Back off, Pete. Let go of my arm!"

"I wasn't anywhere near the house when Sandra went back in. Isn't it clear to you there's got to be someone else here on the island?"

"There can't be. We searched everywhere. All I know is, all these years I've covered for what you did to that girl at the party. And you and I are the last ones left alive who know about it. You've got nothing to lose if you kill me. But that's not going to happen."

Pete looked at her in horror. "Then you know?"

"I've always known. Why do you think I was so anxious not to have the police come to that house? I know you gave her a second tab of ecstasy. I saw you fucking her while she was high on drugs. I watched you screwing her while she wasn't able to speak or defend herself. It was you, Pete! You ruined everything for everybody."

"It's not true!" he cried. "She was beautiful. She loved me!"

As he lunged for her, Sami Lee's arm went out to meet him. She stabbed him once, felt the knife go in, then pulled back and stabbed him a second time. She saw Pete's surprised expression turn to a twisted sneer as he looked down at his bloody chest.

"Bitch," he said.

He fell to the ground.

"Now you're absolved of your sins," she told him.

She pulled the knife out. Blood spewed onto the sand from the two gaping wounds in his chest. Pete gave a final gurgling gasp and lay still.

CHAPTER 27

Sami Lee left Pete lying there and went back into the house. They were all gone now, so there was nothing left to fear. The facade of strength she had maintained since Max's death quickly began to crumble. She went into the bathroom and turned on the water, lit several candles, and ceremoniously laid the knife out on the edge of the tub.

She looked at herself in the mirror and saw the horrors of flesh staring back at her. She had lived too long. She was fifty-six. Getting old and ugly was not the proper way for the true love of a rock legend to end her life. Therefore, she would die beautifully and make up for the too many years she'd endured in poverty and ignominy. Nothing else could atone for having lived too long except to arrange for a beautiful death. And that was one thing Sami Lee knew well how to do.

She stripped off her clothes and placed the recorder on the tiles beside the bathtub. She pressed On and slipped into the water. Then, slowly, she began to talk, describing the knife as it cut into her wrists, telling the mechanical ear how quickly the blood ran from the veins as the candles swayed on the far side of the room. She kept talking, describing how the tub filled up with red, as she let the knife drop to the floor, her voice getting weaker and weaker till finally it was heard no more.

In her last few conscious moments, she thought about Yoko Ono and how she too had been blamed for the end of a legendary band, even blamed for John's assassination because it was she who had convinced him to move to New York and the Dakota Apartments where he lived out his final days. Would they think it was Sami Lee's fault for bringing Max to Shark Island? No matter, it couldn't be helped now. She thought of Janis Joplin's sad ending in a Hollywood hotel, overdosing on heroin a week after Jimi Hendrix died. She thought of Sid and Nancy, and all the other legends who came to a tragic end. Finally, she thought of Pamela Morrison, another rock widow whose husband had loved and betrayed her with both men and women, as well as drugs, and finally death. Jim too had escaped, leaving Pam behind until she could stand it no more and took her own life. And so Sami Lee said goodbye to this mortal plane, taking with her all her secrets and pains, her private sorrows and memories.

Some time later, the recording came to an end with a tiny final click. And some time after that, the candles burned down one by one and the room went dark.

Outside, the sun was shining brightly over the island.

CHAPTER 28

The police report was aided by the tape recorder found beside the bathtub with the body of the dead Asian woman. Narrated at first by a soft male voice, and later by what the police concluded was the voice of the dead woman in the bathtub, it detailed daily events on the island as well as the confessions of eleven people involved in the overdose of a young woman at a house party in Seattle's market district twenty years before.

The confessions were first- or at times second-hand accounts, given by the combined group of eleven who expired on the island. (So the police concluded, once the bodies were counted and the names and details of the individuals summed up.) As far as the police were able to determine, all confessions were given freely and of the victims' own accord. Nothing seemed to have been coerced.

From what they could tell, the first on the island to die was a Guyanese-born lawyer named Noni Embrem, age forty-eight. His confession consisted of an admission that he had once bribed a drug dealer named Newt Merton to plead no contest to manslaughter charges over the death of a Ladykillers fan after Noni promised Newt he would receive a suspended sentence. Newt accepted the bribe, but went to jail for the crime while the others went free. His death was determined to have been the result of ingesting poison in a cocktail mixed by the retreat's chef, Jack Edwards.

Second to die was Janice Sandford, a.k.a. Sarah Wynberg, forty-nine, host of the party where the young fan, Zerin Ames, had been given an overdose of ecstasy. Her confession, not caught on tape but spoken privately to a nurse, concerned the fact that she had been having sex with the dead girl's date, Spike Anthrax. As a result, no one noticed when the girl went into convulsions caused by the overdose. At the time of the trial, Wynberg denied allegations about her involvement, as well as the involvement of the others in the girl's death, claiming Ames had left the party with friends. Like Embrem, she, too, had been poisoned, in her case via medication administered by the island nurse, Sandra Goodman. Wynberg's confession was later narrated and confirmed on tape by Goodman herself.

As far as could be discerned, the likely third death was that of a forty-seven-year-old man employed to ferry the guests back and forth. He had gone by the name of Jack Edwards, though he had many aliases known to the police. Edwards's part in Ames's death occurred when he was unwittingly asked to take her to a hospital in his taxi cab. He was never formally accused in the investigation, although it was on record at the taxi company dispatch that he had dropped Ames off at the emergency ward. Edwards apparently drowned when his boat disintegrated, possibly as a result of the severity of the storm. His may have been the only natural death among the eleven, though given the circumstances of the others, the police were unwilling to rule out homicide.

A fourth guest, a real-estate agent named David, a.k.a. "Newt" Merton, forty-six, died of electrocution when he attempted to plug in a faulty fridge that had been deliberately tampered with. According to Merton's confession, both at the trial and on the island, he had supplied the drugs at the party where the girl received a bad dose of ecstasy. In his defence, Merton claimed that another dealer had tampered with his supplies in an attempt to put him out of business.

The fifth and sixth bodies belonged to rock musicians Max Hardcore and Spike Anthrax, both fifty, and both former members of the punk-rock group known as the Ladykillers. Hardcore died from a suspicious fall over a third-floor railing some time on the night of the third day; his former partner, Spike, died of a lethal injection of methamphetamines the following morning. Their parts in the death of Ames were substantiated on tape as well. Anthrax had invited the girl to the party, but quickly abandoned her for the hostess, Sarah Wynberg. He and Hardcore had apparently been the two men who took the dying Ames out to the taxi operated by Edwards. They left her with Edwards, along with a note saying she had taken an overdose of ecstasy, directing him to take her to the nearest hospital.

Although Ames made it to the hospital by cab, she was simply dropped off by Edwards, who failed to notify the on-call nurse. The note stating details of her condition was subsequently misplaced, which may have contributed to her demise. Again, this confession was not given on tape by Edwards, but by the real estate agent, David Merton, who claimed Edwards had confessed his part in the affair to him privately.

A footnote to the report stated it might be worth mentioning that, while it likely went unknown to the eleven victims, another murder occurred the same week as the island fatalities. The death of the band's former manager, Harvey Keill, fifty-four, also seems to corroborate claims made on tape by several of the victims who felt they were being targeted as revenge for the death of Zerin Ames in a way that accorded with the lyrics of a Ladykillers song, "The Twelve Days of Shagging," in which each of the twelve days is marked by a gift of something potentially lethal.

The first of these, "a love letter full of hate," would in fact concur with this thesis, as Keill was believed to have died from ingesting a poisonous substance mailed to him some days before the others arrived on the island. The sender was anonymous, but the envelope contained a CD with a bootleg copy of the song, in which the poison was hidden.

The eighth known death was that of Crispin LaFey, fifty-three. LaFey, who suffered from near-blindness, was a well-known and much-respected rock critic. He was reportedly writing a compendium on the history of punk rock, and had attended the Ladykillers' reunion in hopes of obtaining some first-hand accounts. He was found with a fully functional laptop at his bedside. A full pack of insulin vials lay tucked inside one of the flaps. No trace of a manuscript or any sort of notes on what occurred on the island was found on the computer, however.

LaFey's death was considered one of the larger mysteries, in that he appeared to have died of an insulin overdose, though the tape mentioned the disappearance of his insulin at a critical period. However, the islanders believed he died from poison injected by the nurse, Sandra. Traces of an unusual chemical compound were found in his body, though its makeup was not confirmed. While fully clothed when he was discovered, it was noted that one of LaFey's socks had been removed and left lying on the floor beside his bed. An additional oddity was that of an empty syringe found protruding from the door of the room occupied by the body of Spike Anthrax, directly across the hall from LaFey's.

At this point, the recorded narrative was taken over by the woman named Sami Lee, fifty-six. Her voice on the tape, as one police officer put it, "was eerie and spooky, full of malice and spite." She could be heard calling herself "Keeper of the Ladykillers Legacy," and seemed to have been determined to follow the events on the island to their conclusion. According to the tape, she was the last person alive, which would point to her as the obvious murderer of most, if not all, of those on the island. There were, however, several reasons to refute this, of which more was noted in a postscript.

The ninth victim was the transsexual, Verna Temple, thirty-nine. As indicated in medical records kept of everyone on the island, Temple was allergic to wasp stings. She was found dead in her bedroom with the remains of a wasps' nest on the floor. It appeared that an attempt to intervene in the wasp attack was stymied by the fact that Temple's door was locked on the inside and the key was not immediately available, for reasons as yet unknown. However, it seemed that when the last three guests broke into her room they found both the window and door locked from inside, leaving no possible explanation as to how the nest ended up in the room. It was later determined that it was pushed in through a small vent near the room's ceiling, possibly while she was asleep.

According to the taped recounting, the following morning the final three victims — Sami Lee, Sandra Goodman, and Pete Doghouse — left the house to try to attract the attention of a passing boat. At some point, Goodman, forty-four, returned to the house to retrieve materials for burning to further their effort. According to Lee's account, Goodman did not return. Pete Doghouse, forty-nine, went into the house against Lee's wishes. When Lee arrived on the scene, Doghouse claimed that he had found Goodman strangled and laid out on her bed, but denied having killed her. (She was in fact found strangled and in bed, as the police discovered.)

At this point, Lee says Doghouse attacked her. She fought him off with a carving knife, stabbing him twice in the chest and leaving his body on the beach near the cove, where he was found when the police arrived.

This is another of the instances where the taped account directly contradicted the evidence as the police discovered it. When Doghouse's body was found, there were two stab wounds to the chest, as Lee described them, but there was a third wound in his back as well. In fact, Doghouse was found lying on his back impaled on the knife, which was not discovered until his body was turned over. It was later concluded by forensics that it was this same knife that Sami Lee used to commit suicide in the bathtub, though the impossibility of cutting her wrists before stabbing Doghouse a third time, and leaving the knife in his back while returning to the bathroom — all without spilling a drop of her own blood — could not be overstated.

There was also a running narrative explaining how a series of twelve chess pieces were systematically removed, or knocked over, on a chessboard in the drawing room after each murder, up until the death of Temple. Another piece was said to have been placed on the chest of Max Hardcore after his death. On the same tape, Lee describes how she and Goodman watched Doghouse turn over the fourth-last chess piece, a white queen, while declaring he had not killed Temple. There was no mention of any pieces being moved from that point forward, though when police arrived on the scene all twelve pieces had been set upright on the board, suggesting that players could begin to engage in the next game, though with far fewer than the requisite number of pieces. Whether they were placed in this manner by Sami Lee or by an unknown person and, if so, when that was done had not been determined.

Following the deaths of Goodman and Doghouse, Lee described the final set of events from the bathtub as she slit her wrists and watched the blood flow from her veins, with the bath water running in the background. On the recording, a noise like that of a knife falling can also clearly be heard, though the knife, as explained, was found in Doghouse's back when police arrived.

Needless to say, the investigating officers found it an eerie experience listening to the entirety of the recording for anything that might indicate the presence of another person while Sami Lee lay dying, never being quite sure when she breathed her last.

As well, despite her lengthy relationship with Max Hardcore, the autopsy revealed that Lee died a virgin, her hymen intact. A final note indicated that the bathroom door had been locked and bolted from inside, and that the key was found with Lee's clothing, beside the tub, when her body was discovered.

Once the final examination of the eleven bodies on the island had been made (along with Keill's, for a total of twelve), the only possible conclusion was that there had been a thirteenth person on the island, someone who remained unknown and unseen by the others, and who later changed the scenes of the crime to suit his or her purposes, whatever they may have been. The report concluded by saying the case might never be satisfactorily solved. The investigation was thus filed away with the area's other unsolved crimes some two years after the murders occurred.

CHAPTER 29

J ust before the unexpected death of renowned rock critic Crispin LaFey, his editor at the publishing house ArtsOblete received an email from him. That email contained the entire manuscript of LaFey's long-awaited history of punk rock, entitled *Endgame*. The editor was shocked when, two days later, he learned of the death of his contracted writer. Knowing the editing process would necessarily be a long and painful one, he shelved the manuscript till he might find the strength to delve into its long-awaited treasures.

Due to a change in the press's editorship, however, the manuscript was not read for a number of years after its receipt and then only by chance, as the book had been deleted from the list of pending publications, such being the fate of many worthy manuscripts, shunted from editor to editor, before finding their final destination at the bottom of the recycling bin, never to see the light of day.

Here is the final chapter of that book in its entirety:

DEATH OF THE LADYKILLERS —
Their Tragic, Final Days

I am not a cruel man, though by the end of this narrative some of you may find that hard to accept. I simply ask you to take my word for it and leave it at that. By the time this reaches your eyes, I will already have shuffled off this mortal coil and will be well beyond the reach of any complaints.

Some of you will understand what this narrative contains, but others will be shocked and even scandalized. So be it. This is an account of the last days of Spike Anthrax, Max Hardcore, and Pete Doghouse, the three remaining members of the punk-rock group Ladykillers, a group once billed as "the original bad boys of west coast punk."

Spike and Max were, musically speaking, more like an overblown Keith Richards and Mick Jagger of their time, though I gather they believed themselves to be the Johnny Rotten and Sid Vicious of the United States. In fact, they were nothing of the sort. They were, however, vile and loathsome creatures, and their reckoning had been a long time coming. Let the fearful turn back now.

The Ladykillers died as they lived: a repugnant death suited to rapists, murderers, and other human garbage. Though in my estimation they appeared to have mellowed with age, they were far short of being truly repentant for their actions, and were uniformly outraged to be fingered for a crime so far in the past they no doubt expected it would be forgotten for all time.

This will not be a long chapter in all, as the Ladykillers were of only passing importance to punk rock in particular and to rock music in general. To put it bluntly, what little talent they had consisted of ripping off other more famous bands — not just their sound and their songs, but their looks, attitudes, and media exhibitionism.

When the group met John Lydon, better known to the world as Johnny Rotten, he is reputed to have passed judgment on them with the line, "They're not punk — just spunk." It was an anecdote guitarist Max Hardcore liked to repeat.

In fact, I doubt they even met Lydon and his gang, but for that I have no proof. What I did finally manage to acquire proof of was their involvement in the death of rock groupie Zerin Ames. Just as I am not a cruel man, I am also not given to sentiment, but since its occurrence the death of Ames has haunted me more than any other tragedy I have been associated with in my life. Know this: Ames was a sweet-tempered girl who grew up in a sheltered family in Montana and who should have led a long and happy life. Instead, she had the misfortune to meet up with the Ladykillers when she was invited — by me, sadly — to attend one of their concerts.

(A note to my editor: Of what does this aforementioned proof consist, you will ask? In this case, the personal confessions of the individuals in question, all of which are on a hidden file in my laptop computer. If anyone wants them, the password is "Shark." You will likely find this instrument in the hands of the

Puget Sound Police Force. In good writerly fashion, I have left the name of the likeliest investigating officer at the end of this missive. If in fact he turns out not to be the investigating officer, I am sure he will happily refer you to the officer in question. I found him most amenable while implementing plans for the building of my island retreat.)

But back to the narrative. If you are like me, you may feel that the Ladykillers' hit, "The Twelve Days Of Shagging," evinces a deplorable lack of talent and originality. It did provide, however, a unique opportunity for me to exact revenge on the twelve people responsible for the death of a young woman who had everything to look forward to in life.

London UK councillor Bernard Brook Partridge once said that groups like the Sex Pistols would be "vastly improved" by sudden death. Sadly, not even such an event could have improved the Ladykillers much, in my estimation. In defence of punk music and its many fans, however, I can say with certainty that very few of them, apart from Sid Vicious when he was high on speed, were actually violent. In fact, most were simply intent on having fun, despite their intimidating appearances.

As for a concerted ethos of violence, that was simply an expression of dislike for a status quo that kept them out when they felt, rightly or wrongly, that they had something relevant to contribute to society as a whole. It was that which most exacerbated their anger.

In England, of course, punk was a legitimate expression of lower-class, disaffected youth, while to many it sounded and looked like nothing short of a full-scale rebellion. In fact, it was a refusal to take anything seriously by those who themselves had not been taken seriously. At the time, it meant cutting through the overwhelming weight of class structure and tradition, of which England was dying a slow death. "We're here!" it shouted. "And fuck you if you don't like us, 'cause we sure as hell don't like you, either."

Joe Strummer likened punk music to an earthquake, a natural, uncontrollable, and entirely unpredictable force of destruction. But not all the destruction was obvious. Some of it occurred behind closed doors. This was very true in North America, where punk rock was seen largely as a cultural oddity, little more than a display of bad manners, harsh sounds, and funny-looking clothing held together by safety pins, rather than a legitimate social movement.

But back to the task at hand. I had the first glimmer of my plan for revenge in August of 1999, when former Ladykiller drummer Kent Stabber died of an overdose of heroin, his drug of choice. It was an ugly death, by all accounts, though not necessarily deserved. I understood that Stabber was the one member of the group not at the party where Ames died, and so was never on my "Greatest Hits" list of people to be exterminated. What Stabber's death did was remind me that time was passing and that I needed to act if I were to exact my revenge.

The following month I purchased Shark Island from the government. It was a failed place for unnamed experiments and came with an aura of fear and mystery built into its reputation. In short, it was perfect for my plan.

I had the house built to my specifications over a period of several years and at considerable cost. It had to be built in stages so that I could pay for its progress. Never once did I consider that I might be throwing money away for the wrong reasons. In fact, the more research I did into the various individuals I intended to lure there for their final days, the more convinced did I become of the worthiness of my quest.

Of course, many will remember me as a blind critic, but back then I still had a reasonable degree of sight, which I put to use in drawing my blueprints. When the house was finally completed, I could still see well enough to know I had created my own masterpiece, as it were.

I'd already spent several years building my case against the individuals in question, learning their likes and dislikes, their medical histories and weaknesses. In short, I created files on them that the CIA might well envy.

As my house of assignation came close to being finished, I sent invitations to each of the twelve guilty, with the intention of luring them to the island. First I hired Edwards, the taxi driver and sometime criminal involved in Ames's death. Finding him was a matter of bribing a certain taxi dispatcher who had sent Edwards to the pickup that night.

Next, I hired Sandra Goodman, the former nurse who was absolved of her role in giving an overdose of medication to the dying Zerin Ames, then fresh out of prison. It was only later, on the island, that I learned of her additional connection with the drug supplier, David "Newt" Merton, in supplying him with the raw products for his "party martinis." By the time my plan was set in motion, both Edwards and Goodman had such spotty work histories that I knew they would accept my rather lucrative invitation to join us on the island.

The only one I had worries about accepting was Harvey Keill, a lazy, predatory bastard. In fact, Harvey was the one who could have ruined things by being there, as the band members found him so odious and such an obvious and well-deserved target for dislike that I decided to dispatch him at a distance before the games could begin. I sent Harvey a letter with a CD case dusted in anthrax. A "love letter full of hate," as it were.

The poetic justice of Noni Embrem's choice of drink struck me when I reviewed the lyrics of "The Twelve Days of Shagging" and discovered that the second gift listed was two "silver bullets." I was overjoyed when Noni requested his favourite drink at our very first dinner on the island.

Janice Sandford, a.k.a. Sarah Wynberg, proved another easy target, with her neuroses and her insomnia. She could have been the original model for Dylan's "Just Like A Woman," though she would only have been two years old at the time it was recorded. After Embrem's death, she lost no time asking for something to help with her headache. Sandra ably provided her with the third gift of "evil Jujubes" from the medical case I had prepared with mislabelled vials, among other things.

I knew Edwards would clear out in an effort to save his own skin once he saw the writing on the wall. While he served dinner that night, I misdirected him several times with text messages purportedly from Harvey Keill. In fact, these were sent from within the house. By then Edwards had done as I asked and stolen all remaining cellphones so that no further communication was possible. Except for my second cellphone, of course. Once Noni Embrem died, I was able to slip into his room when the others were asleep that night and retrieve his phone, which Edwards had missed.

Edwards had hidden all the others in a locked cupboard in the kitchen where I stored a quantity of oxalic acid, which I fully intended the others to find along with the cellphones, minus the batteries. This last point nearly proved Edwards's undoing, as Max Hardcore was outside smoking a joint when the otherwise redoubtable Edwards went out into the rain to toss the batteries into the cove. Max eventually decided what he had seen was not Edwards, but Keill, already on the island. This, in fact, served my purpose just as well, for it instilled fear in the others. Later, when it was clear that Harvey wasn't on the island,

Max decided it was the stray dog Spike had seen on his first search of the grounds.

But back to Edwards. Despite what the others believed, he was the fourth to die, in accordance with the song's lyrics ("four oceans to drown in"), though his body was not discovered till the following day. During a break in the proceedings, I was able to sneak down to the boathouse under cover of darkness and splash a quantity of glue-destroying acid on the bottom of the boat. Since the storm had deposited a considerable amount of water in the vessel, and as Edwards was in a panic when he left, he wouldn't have realized until he was some way out into the ocean where the waves were strongest that the boat was literally disintegrating around him. I'm sure his last moments were particularly unpleasant when he realized he'd been tricked into killing himself by abandoning the others, just as he once abandoned Zerin Ames. More poetry.

David "Newt" Merton was next on my list. A near-fatal accident by one of the construction workers provided the key to his death, when I discovered how easy it was to rig an electrical receptacle to make it deadly. Newt accommodated my wishes by plugging the refrigerator back in without taking time to note that the receptacle was faulty. If he had seen the pair of rubber dish gloves on the counter where I left them when I unplugged it, he might have thought twice before grabbing the plug, but he was not particularly observant.

In his younger days, Newt was known for taking chances. He once jumped, while stoned, from the balcony of a twenty-sixth-story apartment across to another railing some four feet away, and then back again. He was a reckless, devil-may-care sort, but this was one live-wire act he didn't survive. If he'd had any decency, he would have tried his supposedly "quality" drugs himself before selling them. Zerin Ames may not have been his only victim, but we may never know of the others who suffered because of his carelessness. To him was bequeathed the gift of "five tongues of fire."

Max always wanted to be a high-flyer, so I gave him his wish to attain the heights once more before he died. His "six bombers diving" was a short-lived flight, however. In fact, I wasn't sure if three stories would be adequate to do him in, but with his weight he hit the floor rather hard. It was unnecessary for me to go downstairs to complete the job. In fact, I had just come up from changing the chessboard once again. That was the most dangerous moment of the entire plan, for in my near-blindness I had knocked over a vase, which shattered rather loudly on the floor. Still, I accomplished what I needed to without being discovered.

With Max dead, I wanted Spike to follow soon thereafter. The poetic justice of the pair dying in close proximity was too much to resist. I simply waited till I had a chance to drug the bowl of cocaine to knock him out.

(He'd used it several times and got sloppy, thinking it safe.) I then crept up behind him and stabbed him in the jugular with one of my insulin needles, the "seven crystals shining," except that it contained a highly lethal mix of crystal meth cut with Drano. I'd had vague qualms about whether or not I would be able to see him well enough to do this, but in fact his tell-tale green hair made it easy to locate him, even when the rest of him was little more than a blurry outline to my dying eyes.

At this point, with the paranoia setting in, things got trickier. The connection between the chess game (my favourite board game) and the murders was by now all too obvious. (Pete was good at keeping the others informed, thanks to his private inner voices.) There was still some doubt about the connection to the song's lyrics, however. If the survivors had looked a little more closely at the words, it might have given them greater insight into what fate would befall them.

With my own "death" imminent, the timing of everything that followed was crucial. In the course of my investigations, I had discovered a book by a Canadian researcher who claimed that stories of zombies in the Caribbean islands were indeed based on fact. I paid a good deal to discover the right amount of the various compounds used, including the venom from a blowfish, among other ingredients designed to stop all outward signs of bodily activity for a short period of time. This required an extremely careful setup, as I first had to take a potentially lethal dosage of the drug.

Immediately prior, I swallowed a quantity of charcoal and ash made from burned fish bones, which had caused some consternation on its discovery in the kitchen around the time Spike Anthrax died. This was intended as part of the resuscitation process, helping to remove the poison by absorbing toxic materials in the body. I then swallowed a lethal dose of the blowfish venom, which made me seem to be having an insulin reaction. At the same time, I convinced Sandra to inject me with an antidote that I had placed in the emergency medical kit. This allowed me to appear dead for several hours. That way, I was fairly sure, I would awaken in due course after my "eight poisoned needles," as I in fact did.

Verna Temple's death proved one of my greatest challenges and biggest triumphs. I knew she was allergic to wasps, and so I enticed a hive to build in my eaves last summer. At the time of building, I had the workers put in an access point to the vent in Verna's room, connecting it with my own, right next door. At night, when I was in my element, so to speak, I was able to manoeuvre the nest into Verna's room. Being woken so discourteously, the "nine wasps a-stinging" were no doubt eager to wreak revenge on the nearest target, in this case, Verna. From the little I could see, the marks on her body were quite in keeping with her various enhancement surgeries, particularly her "bee-stung lips." By the time the others had broken down the door, the deed was done.

While the others believed Sandra's injection the previous day had killed me, it in fact saved my life. I returned the favour by strangling her the following morning when she came to check on my "dead" body. Although I'd shown all the obvious signs of death, I knew that Sandra, being a nurse, would eventually start to get curious after realizing another person had to be on the island. That person, in fact, was me. As Sandra leaned over me to check for signs of breathing, I reached up and throttled her, then laid her out on her own bed for the others to find. "Ten stranglers strangling."

From then on, it was simply a matter of time before Pete and Sami Lee turned on one another. They shared a life-long hatred, and leaving them to deal with each other at the end pleased me a great deal. From the upstairs window, I followed their movements down by the water. I watched as Pete returned to the house and discovered Sandra's body. He reported this to Sami Lee, who by then was convinced that her arch-enemy Pete was the real killer. With his crazy voices, he was a nat-ural for the role. "Eleven stabbers stabbing."

I'm not sure which of them I despised most, in fact. Pete for giving Zerin Ames the drug overdose and later raping her while she lay dying, or Sami Lee for her selfish decision to hide the truth from the world.

After that, it was simply a matter of waiting. I knew that without Max, Sami Lee would kill herself. "Twelve suicides." If she hadn't, I would happily have done it for her. I have said that my blindness enhanced my sense of smell. It also enhanced my hearing. It was pure serendipity when I heard the knife she used to slit her wrists fall on the bathroom mat, which I was able to retrieve under the sill. I was also able to listen as, true to her controlling nature, Sami Lee did a superb job of having the last word — apart from this one, of course.

Later, I took the knife Sami Lee stabbed Pete with and went back out to give him the final blow. I felt it was my due. How I wish it had been the killing blow, but it was a symbolic victory at least, to stab him in the back and leave his body on the beach with the knife embedded in his flesh.

How confusing that will be for the local police force when they discover that the last one standing was not the killer of all those who died before her, but merely the killer of the one person she hated most.

As for myself, I have little time left no matter the outcome. The retina blastoma that has destroyed my eyesight has since spread to my other organs. I have at best only a month or two before I'll die of natural causes. Ending things this way, I feel, is far superior.

I have just reset the twelve chess pieces on the board. In a few moments, once I send this email off to my publishers, I will tie a sock as a tourniquet around my left leg and inject myself with an overdose of insulin, retrieved from my computer bag. (In case you're wondering, I hid it underneath Spike's dead body. It was slim enough that no one noticed it there.) As a final gesture of defiance, I will throw the used syringe at the door opposite mine, Spike's room. With any luck, it will hang quivering on the door, where no doubt the police will find it when they arrive.

At that time, my deeds all but over, I will lie down on my bed and release the tourniquet, one white sock, which will not look too out of place along with everything else lying scattered around me. Having accomplished that, I will breathe my last.

And so, my friends, that is the end of the sad saga of the Ladykillers and one of the final chapters of punk-rock music.

I hereby bid you adieu.

Yours faithfully,

Crispin LaFey

ACKNOWLEDGEMENTS

First and foremost, I offer thanks to the ever-resourceful Dame Agatha Christie for the endless hours of fascination and bloodless detection her ingenuity has provided me and countless other readers. I would be remiss not to say thanks once again to my illustrious editor, Shannon Whibbs, whose suggestions always help to "enhance the natural." Cheers also to Allison Hirst, James Hatch, Laura Boyle, Synora Van Drine, and all the good folks at Dundurn who make my job pretty cool. A nod goes out to Ryan McConnell, Erin Howe, and members of that fab band, These Electric Lives, whose hijinks set my inspiration buzzing, as well as to Shane McConnell, David Tronetti, and Enrique García-Pereña.

ALSO BY JEFFREY ROUND

Lake on the Mountain
A Dan Sharp Mystery

Winner of the 2013 Lambda Award for Best Gay Mystery

Dan Sharp, a gay father and missing-persons investigator, accepts an invitation to a wedding on a yacht in Ontario's Prince Edward County. It seems just the thing to bring Dan closer to his noncommittal partner, Bill, a respected medical professional with a penchant for sleazy after-hours clubs, cheap drugs, and rough sex. But the event doesn't go exactly as planned. When a member of the wedding party is swept overboard, a case of mistaken identity leads to confusion as the wrong person is reported missing. The hunt for a possible killer leads Dan deeper into the troubled waters and private lives of a family of rich WASPs and their secret world of privilege. No sooner is that case resolved when a second one ends up on Dan's desk. Dan is hired by an anonymous source to investigate the disappearance, twenty years earlier, of the groom's father. The only clues are a missing bicycle and six horses mysteriously poisoned.

Pumpkin Eater
A Dan Sharp Mystery

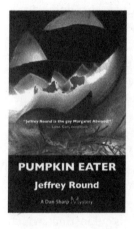

In the second Dan Sharp Mystery, missing-persons investigator Dan Sharp makes a grisly find in a burned-out slaughterhouse in Toronto's west end after following an anonymous tip. Someone is targeting known sex offenders whose names and identities were released on the Internet. When an iconic rock star contacts Dan to keep from becoming the next victim, things take a curious turn. Dan's search for a killer takes him underground in Toronto's broken social scene — a secret world of misfits and guerrilla activists living off the grid — where he hopes to find the key to the murders.

The Jade Butterfly
A Dan Sharp Mystery

A seemingly casual encounter in a downtown bar sends missing-persons investigator Dan Sharp in search of a woman presumed dead in the Tiananmen Square Massacre. Twenty years after her disappearance, her brother believes that a woman he glimpsed on the Internet is his sister, now living in Toronto. The closer Dan gets to finding her, however, the less sense things make. Just when he thinks he knows what's driving his client, an unexpected revelation forces him to choose between what he's been told and his gut instinct, which says things are not all they seem.

Available at your favourite bookseller

VISIT US AT
Dundurn.com
@dundurnpress
Facebook.com/dundurnpress
Pinterest.com/dundurnpress